The Crooked Mirror
and Other Stories

ANTON CHEKHOV IN 1883

THE
CROOKED MIRROR
AND OTHER STORIES
❖ ❖ ❖

by

ANTON CHEKHOV

Translated and with an Introduction by
ARNOLD HINCHLIFFE

ZEBRA BOOKS
KENSINGTON PUBLISHING CORP.

ZEBRA BOOKS

are published by

Kensington Publishing Corp.
475 Park Avenue South
New York, NY 10016

First Zebra Books printing: May, 1992
0-8217-3733-3
Printed in the United States of America

CONTENTS

❖ ❖ ❖

Illustrations

INTRODUCTION

❖ ❖ ❖

ANTON CHEKHOV WROTE THESE STORIES IN HIS TWENTIES, when he was a student at Moscow University and later a practising doctor. In these years he wrote three hundred or more stories, and as many satirical pieces, parodies, crime reports, theatre critiques, jokes and journalistic odds and ends—mostly for money: he was the chief support of his father and mother, his brothers and his sister, living as best they could in a four-room basement in a dingy, disreputable sub-urb—and almost always in a hurry.

Yet the quality of some of this early work is remarkable. It includes some of the finest short stories ever written ("Mis-ery"; "The Trick").

A wealth of avid experience was behind the writing. His formative years in Taganrog had been rich in manifold impres-sions. The third child of six—five sons and a daughter—he was the bright observer of a turbulent household, who resisted the tyranny and heavy piety of his father by quietly not giving in, and comforted his sensitive mother by his ever-ready pres-ence. He worked busy hours in his father's shop—part grocery, part herbal store, part tavern—and so became acquainted with a whole range of poor purchasers, sailors, peasants, small traders, cadgers, street people. But he also enjoyed life, loved listening to his mother's stories, played games with his brothers and sisters, got up charades and family theatricals, was sometimes off for days into the country or along the seashore. "I love merry-making," he would later write, "particularly Russian merry-making."

When his father faced bankruptcy in Taganrog and fled with the family to Moscow, young Anton, aged 16, was told: "Stay here. Finish your studies and shift for yourself." He lived for a time in the sold family home and paid for his keep by giving lessons to the new owner's son. He made a little money by selling off the old family pots and pans. Occasionally he moved in with friends, then moved on. He tried his hand at some trivial unrewarding journalism, undertook many odd jobs, even winged goldfinches with birdshot to sell them in the market. "I am well," he wrote to a younger brother, "and that means I am alive. I have only one secret illness which torments me like an aching tooth—lack of money." He already had insight into life at the rough edges, knew how to survive.

Despite his poverty and the hard grind of his existence he managed to be accepted in local society, to make friends, visit the theatre and music hall, go shooting and fishing, live for a time on a Cossack farm, learn to ride. He was already sexually precocious. He later told his friend that his first sexual experience was at the age of 13.

He even sent a little money to his family in Moscow, in reply to letters from his mother, telling him how hard their life was.

He also had been close to death. One hot summer day he swam in a cold river and fell seriously ill with peritonitis. A Russo-German doctor called Strempf saved his life. As he recovered, Anton decided that he too would become a doctor.

He achieved sufficient qualifications in his examination to enter the medical faculty of Moscow University; he was not quite twenty years old, but now with a cool independence which belied his years, and a tough sense of responsibility to the family. He was a young man who had come through.

He found the family in Moscow in dire need. His father was between jobs; his elder brothers, Alexander, a writer, and Nikolai, a painter, were more in need of help than able to provide it and both had drinking problems; and his younger brothers and his sister were still adolescent. All that was visible from their damp basement was the roadway and the feet of passers-by; and sometimes when the entire family was at home, and there had been drinking and singing, they all slept as they were, on a vast mattress on the floor, their dog finding a comfortable place among them.

Anton had a scholarship of twenty-five roubles a month from the Taganrog town council, and he brought two school-friends with him, also medical students, and his mother took them in as boarders in two of the basement rooms. Alexander and Nikolai moved out and fended for themselves, and their father obtained work at a wholesale warehouse and had, in effect, to live there. This made Anton the real head of the family. His youngest brother Michael wrote: "Anton has taken the place of father, and father's personality has receded into the background."

Desperately in need of money, Anton studied the comic stories in Moscow and Petersburg papers and magazines and then submitted his own. The first to be accepted was in January 1880, about the time of his twentieth birthday. Others soon followed. In search of material Anton went here and there in Moscow, meeting an enormous variety of people. But he kept his new profession fairly secret, writing under an assumed name, usually that of Antosha Chekhonte.

He had to write all the time, even when he took the family on holiday in the summer.

"My family lives with me, cooking, baking and roasting whatever I can afford to buy with the money I earn by writing. Life isn't too bad."

Soon he was able to move the family into quarters in a better district. Which meant the need for money increased.

He wrote hurriedly—"Write, write, write till your fingers break. . . Don't be disturbed by rejections. Write a story at one go." And, as he said later, he wrote "mechanically, half-consciously, as reporters write their notices of a fire."

The bulk of his work was still comic stories. He dismissed many of them as trash. Then, as Antosha Chekhonte became more widely known, he wrote sad and bitter stories too, stories of social protest, of acute psychological perception. And the humour became sharper, astringent, deeply ironical. By now he was, I think, a compulsive writer, like his Trigorin in *The Seagull*: "I write ceaselessly, as if hurrying post haste, and I can't do otherwise." And his quick thought evoked vividly the feel of life experienced sharply on the nerve at a given moment.

A giant of a man grapples, face to face, with a wolf: "Both of them, Nilov and the wolf, their heads level now, looked each other in the eyes . . . The wolf snapped its teeth, made a squeaky sound and slavered . . . Its back legs, seeking support, knocked against Nilov's knees . . . The moon lit up its eyes, but there was nothing vicious to see there; they seemed to be weeping, like a human being's." ("The Wolf")

Rebrotyesov remembers a dish of sturgeon: "So savoury was his memory of that sturgeon that the garrison commander sniffed suddenly the smell of fish and chewed unconsciously, not noticing that mud was gathering in his galoshes." ("Tears the World Does Not See")

Iona, the sledgeman, is heavy with grief: "Let his heart break and misery flow out, then it would flood the whole world so it seems; and yet it is not seen. It is lodged in such an unimportant shell, you couldn't find it with a candle in the daylight." ("Misery")

This was, I think, his starting point—a sense of life as immediate experience—from which he moved deeper, analysing the response of his characters to the experience. And here the fact that he began as a comic writer—and would always claim to be such—is important. He directed his attention to the points of comic stress, where human folly and weakness are. He saw the ironical pattern in the ordinary, the man behind the rank, the dream behind the posture—a henpecked husband in a garrison commander, a frustrated would-be father in a philanderer—the comedy, indeed, behind the tragedy.

And in the sad, bitter and satirical stories the approach was the same. The tensions came at the points of stress where thought and action are at variance, illusion entangled with reality. There is a sharpening of perception by irony, a method of deep comedy that Chekhov made his own.

It is a method which gives insight into human love. How many of Chekhov's stories are about lovers or about those who need love, because it is at the point of irony, of human weakness, that the need is. Iona, the old sledgeman, is weighed down by such need, all meaning gone; Nadia, the victim of "The Trick" retains all her life an illusion of a great love; and the "Tears the World Does Not See" are those of Rebrotyesov loving the wife who henpecks him. (And who knows? Perhaps in her pecking there is a kind of love: "Give me my dress from the chair, Mahomet!")

Because Chekhov's comic method has not been widely appreciated—particularly in the West—his early stories have been neglected. This collection will show how fine some of them are.

On the other hand, we must not overrate. The splendid work emerged from a mass of journalistic material, much of it frothy and shallow. There was light entertainment, sheer fun, some rough-hewn drama. Much of the greater work was clearly to come. Chekhov developed and refined his method of deep comedy as he shaped his later masterpieces. It became wiser, sharper, more evocative, it incorporated a kind of poetry which gave a greater intimacy of feeling with his people and a clearer understanding of their world: yet its essence remained the same.

But the finest early stories are still a source of wonder. (The other great short-story writers—Pushkin, Tolstoy, Turgenev, Flaubert, Maupassant, Stevenson, Conrad, Henry James—matured later, some much later, and they were from a background of literature, not from brief years of hack-writing under pressure.) How did this young man understand so deeply the middle-aged arty globe-trotters of "He and She," have sure knowledge of their devoted love despite bitter conflict, hysteria on her part, cruelty on his? Or know the secret fears of the feckless prostitute of "A Gentleman Friend" who endures the extraction of a healthy tooth, because, in a new setting, she is afraid to ask an old client for money? How did he see life, as it were, from within the skin of the peasant dwarf of "He Understood" who kills from "yearning sadness"? And know the emotions of the giant in "The Wolf," always too big for where he is standing, screaming in fear, but a little later laughing with joy, carrying off a doctor under his arm in sheer delight? (Indeed it is possible that young Chekhov himself was the doctor.)

Imagine the writer, then, as you read his stories: a handsome young man in his twenties, sensitive and deep. He has had a full day as a medical student, and now writes in a house finally quiet after the family have gone to bed. Or they are on holiday, and he is up at the table very early before their morning noises disturb him.

He spent many hours yesterday at his favourite pastime, quiet fishing, or wandering at ease, chewing sunflower seeds like a peasant, brooding on memories for use in this tale.

Imagine him, then, as his thought cuts deep in memory and dream, bringing forth living people, the spontaneous shock and impact of life itself; at his finest he is seeing and recording at the heart of things, where social pressures hurt most and the need for love is.

❖ ❖ ❖

In 1889, when he was nearly thirty, Chekhov experienced a crisis in his work. He had achieved a high reputation—he was Anton Chekhov now, not Antosha Chekhonte—and in 1888 had been awarded the Pushkin Prize by the Russian Academy of Sciences for the quality of his stories. But he was deeply dissatisfied.

"There is a sort of stagnation in my soul!" he wrote. "Somehow everything has suddenly lost interest for me."

He had recently completed "A Boring Story" in which he described the life of a professor who discovers near death that he has lived without purpose: "Each feeling and each thought lives in me separately, and in all my opinions of science, theatre, literature and students and in all the pictures which my imagination draws not even the most skilful analyst could find a ruling idea to serve as a god for a living man. And if that is not there, nothing is there."

The recent death of Chekhov's brother Nikolai, of the illness from which he himself suffered, had had a profound effect. The time left to him seemed suddenly short and he wanted to live it to the full: "In January, I'll be thirty. Hail the old bachelor. Useless life, burn to the end!"

But he desperately wanted his life not to be useless, to have a purpose. It had hurt him when the journal *Russian Thought* called him "an unprincipled writer," and he wrote an angry letter to the editor. He had also come under the influence of Tolstoy and called *The Kreutzer Sonata*, a polemic novel, recently published, a work "unequalled in seriousness of conception." Though it was against Chekhov's nature to state this plainly, he wanted to undertake a formidable task of importance to mankind: "I want to erase a year or a year and a half from my life. . . . I will go where I can study men and women at their most degraded and pitiful."

And so he decided to travel across Siberia to the convict settlements on Sakhalin Island in the Far East, where he would make a full, detailed census and a medical report. It would be a journey of more than four thousand miles by train and ship but mostly by carriage across the immense Siberian plain. He would accomplish it in rather more than two months.

He gave reasons for his decision in a letter to his friend Alexei Suvorin, the editor: men and women were rotting in prison after a cold march in chains across thousands of miles, and this was the concern of all Russians. His only regret was that he was the one to go there and not someone more capable of arousing public interest. He wanted to pay his debt to medicine, which he had neglected for literature. (He used to call medicine his wife and literature his mistress.) He also needed "incessant work, physical and mental," because he was becoming lazy.

But these are rationalizations. His deep motives were psychological. He needed a kind of cleansing of the mind, to let the imagination lie fallow for a time, to record only what he saw and heard and thought and felt. His Siberian diary was a chronicle of pure experience.

And yet the observer was still Anton Chekhov, the creative writer. What he recorded was raw material for later imaginative work when the fallow time was over. The people whom he met were as they were, no more nor less: yet they were the kernels of characters in later works. Is little Sasha, the abandoned child a childless couple have made their own, the Sasha whom Olga, "The Darling" in his famous story of that name, has adopted and so fears to lose?

Chekhov left Moscow on 21 April 1890. He travelled by train to Yaroslavl, then sailed on the Volga and the Kama to Perm, then travelled by train to Ekaterinburg. It was not until he reached Tyumen that he began his journal, *From Siberia*. Between Tyumen and Irkutsk, a journey which lasted most of May and June, he posted episodes to Alexei Suvorin in Moscow, and these were published in nine instalments in *New Time* in June, July and August.

Chekhov reached Sakhalin Island on 11 July and was there until 13 October. He travelled extensively in all kinds of weather, working sometimes from five in the morning until late at night. He interviewed every prisoner and filled in a census card for each, some 10,000 cards of 13 entries each. He accumulated the data he would use for his account of the island and the convict settlements. This account—*Sakhalin Island*—was published in 1893 in *Russian Thought*, the journal which had called him "an unprincipled writer."

Chekhov came home by way of Hong Kong, Singapore and

Ceylon. He wrote to Suvorin: "Before my journey, *The Kreut-zer Sonata* was an event for me, but now I find it ridiculous and foolish. Either I have grown up because of my journey, or I have lost my senses. The devil only knows."

Soon he was writing compulsively again.

Before he departed Chekhov wrote: "Won't the journey give me at least two or three days that I shall remember all my life with joy or grief?"

Almost certainly it did. And more.

BIBLIOGRAPHICAL NOTE

❖ ❖ ❖

"The Crooked Mirror, A Christmas Story" (*"Krivoye zerkalo, Svya-tochny rasskaz"*), published January 1883, in *Spectator (Zriteli)*.

"He and She" (*"On i ona"*), published June 1882 in *Worldly Trend (Mirskoy tolk)*; translation by Frances H. Jones, (Capricorn, 1959).

"Two Scandals" (*"Dva skandala"*), published December 1882, in *Worldly Trend (Mirskoy tolk)*; translation by Nora Gottlieb (Bodley Head, 1961).

"A Woman without Prejudices" (*"Zhenshchina bez predrassud-kov"*), published February 1883, in *Spectator (Zriteli)*.

"He Understood" (*"On ponyal"*), published November 1883, in *Nature and Hunting (Priroda i okhota)*.

"75,000" (*"Sem'desyat pyat tisach"*), published January 1884, in *Alarm Clock (Budelnik)*, translation by Frances H. Jones, (Capricorn, 1959).

"Tears the World Does Not See" (*"Nevidimyie miru slyozy"*), published August 1884, in *Fragments (Oskolki)*. Arnold Hinchliffe's translation appeared in *The Sinner from Toledo and Other Stories* (Cranbury, New Jersey: Associated University Presses, 1972).

"The Mask" (*"Maska"*), published October 1884, in *Entertainment (Razvlechaniye)*; translation by April Fitzlyon and Kyril Zinoviev (British Book Centre, 1952).

"A Terrible Night, A Christmas Story" (*"Strashnaya noch, Svya-tochny rasskaz"*), published December 1884, in *Entertainment (Razvlechaniye)*; translations by Constance Garnett (Chatto & Windus, 1916–1950), by A. E. Chamot (Stanley Paul, 1926), and

Patrick Miles and Harvey Pitcher (1982). Arnold Hinchliffe's translation was broadcast by the B.B.C. London, in 1985.

"The Crow" ("*Vorona*"), published June 1885, in *Fragments (Oskolki)*.

"The Boots" ("*Sapogi*"), published July 1885, in *Petersburg Gazette (Peterburgskaya gazeta)*; translation by Constance Garnett (Chatto & Windus, 1916–1950).

"The Father of a Family" ("*Otets semeystva*"), published September 1885 in *Petersburg Gazette (Peterburgskaya gazeta)*; translation by Marion Fell (Duckworth, 1915), and by Constance Garnett (Chatto & Windus, 1916–1950).

"The Exclamation Mark, A Christmas Story" ("*Vosklitsatel'ny znak, Svyatochny rasskaz*"), published December 1885, in *Fragments (Oskolki)*.

"The Dream, A Christmas Story" ("*Son, Svatochny rasskaz*"), published December 1885, in *Petersburg Gazette (Peterburgskaya gazeta)*.

"The Mirror, A Christmas Story" ("*Zerkalo, Svyatochny rassakas*"), published December 1885, in *Petersburg Gazette (Petersburgskaya gazeta)*.

"Misery" ("*Toska*"), published January 1886, in *Petersburg Gazette (Peterburgskaya gazeta)*; translations by L. Kaye (Heinemann, 1915), and by Constance Garnett (Chatto & Windus, 1916–1950).

"A Night in the Graveyard, A Christmas Story" ("*Noch na kladbishche, Svyatochny rasskaz*"), published January 1886, in *The Cricket (Sverchok)*; translation by Constance Garnett (Chatto & Windus, 1916–1950).

"The Wolf" ("*Volk*"), published March 1886, in *Petersburg Gazette (Peterburgskaya gazeta)*.

"The Trick" ("*Shutochka*"), published March 1886, in *The Cricket (Sverchok)*; translations by Marion Fell (Duckworth, 1915), and by Constance Garnett (Chatto & Windus, 1916–1950). Arnold Hinchliffe's translation appeared in *The Sinner from Toledo and Other Stories* (Cranbury, New Jersey: Associated University Presses, 1972).

"Agafya" ("*Agafya*"), published March 1886, in *New Time (Novoye vremya)*; translations by Marion Fell, (Duckworth, 1915), and Constance Garnett (Chatto & Windus, 1916–1950), and David Magarshack (Penguin Books, 1964).

"A Gentleman Friend" ("Znakomi mushchina"), published May 1886, in Fragments (Oskolki); translations by S. Koteliansky and J. Middleton Murry (Maunsel & Co., 1915), and by Constance Garnett (Chatto & Windus, 1916–1950).

"Love Affair with a Double-Bass" ("Roman s kontrobasom"), published June 1886, in Fragments (Oskolki). Arnold Hinchliffe's translation appeared in The Sinner from Toledo and Other Stories (Cranbury, New Jersey: Associated University Presses, 1972). A dramatized version was broadcast by the B.B.C., London, in 1985.

"A Little Crime" ("Bezzakoniye"), published June 1887, in Fragments (Oskolki); translation by Constance Garnett (Chatto & Windus, 1916–1950).

From Siberia (Iz Sibiri), published June, July, and August 1890, in New Time (Novoye vremya); translation by Avraham Yarmolinsky (Noonday, 1954). Excerpts from Arnold Hinchliffe's translation were published in The London Magazine in 1988.

The Crooked Mirror
and Other Stories

Первая страница рукописи рассказа А. П. Чехова
«Кривое зеркало»   стр. 11

The first page of the original manuscript of "The Crooked Mirror"

THE CROOKED MIRROR
(A CHRISTMAS STORY)

❖ ❖ ❖

WE WENT INTO THE RECEPTION HALL, MY WIFE AND I. IT smelled of moss and damp. Hordes of rats and mice leaped aside as we brought light to walls that had not seen it for a century. As we shut the door behind us, a puff of wind rustled papers piled in corners; light fell on them and we noticed ancient lettering and medieval pictures. On walls green with age hung portraits of my ancestors. They stared down, stern and disdainful, as if about to say:

"A whipping for you, my man!"

Our steps resounded through the building. I coughed and there came an echo, the very one that replied once to my ancestors . . .

And the wind moaned and howled. There was a sobbing in the chimney stack like someone in despair and big drops of rain beat a melancholy patter on the glimmering windows.

"Oh, ancestors of mine," I murmured with a sigh, "if I were a writer, looking at your portraits, I could write a long novel. For each of these old people was young once and each man or woman of them was a fitting subject. And what a story it

I

would be! Look, say, at that old lady, my great-grandmother
That ugly misshapen woman had a remarkable history."

"Do you see the mirror," I asked my wife, "do you see it,
hanging there in the corner?"

And I pointed out to her a large mirror in a frame of black-
ened bronze that hung in a corner near the portrait of my great-
grandmother.

"That mirror has magic powers: it was the ruin of my great-
grandmother. For it she paid an enormous sum and she did
not part with it until the moment of her death. Day and night,
incessantly, she looked into it, looked even when she ate and
drank. As she went to sleep, she laid the mirror by her in the
bed and, dying, begged that it be laid beside her in the coffin.
It was only because it would not fit into the coffin that her
wish was unfulfilled."

"She was a vain coquette, wasn't she?" said my wife.

"I admit it. But hadn't she other mirrors, then? Why was it
just *that* mirror that she loved and not another? Hadn't she
better mirrors even? No, my dear, some terrible secret is hid-
den there. How else do you explain it? Legend has it there's a
devil in the mirror and that my great-grandmother was fasci-
nated by devils."

I brushed dust from the mirror, looked into it and began to
laugh. A dull echo replied. It was a crooked mirror that twisted
my features in all directions: my nose appeared on my left
cheek and my chin was cleft and turned askew.

"What strange tastes my great grandmother had!" I said.

My wife went hesitantly to the mirror and she too glanced
there—and at once a terrible thing happened. She went pale,
trembled all over and cried out. The candlestick dropped from
her hand and rolled on the floor and the candle went out.
Darkness closed over us.

And at that very moment I heard something heavy falling:
my wife had lost consciousness.

The wind moaned on as sadly as ever, rats scampered, mice
rustled among the papers. The hairs bristled and stirred on my

head as a shutter broke from a window and clattered down, and the moon came into view . . .

I lifted my wife in my arms and carried her from the house of my ancestors. And it was not till the evening of the next day that she came to herself.

"The mirror! Give me the mirror!" she said. "Where is the mirror?"

For a full week afterwards she neither ate nor drank nor slept and all the time kept asking for the mirror to be brought to her. She sobbed, tore her hair and tossed to and fro till at last, when the doctor said she might die of exhaustion, her condition being extremely grave, I mastered my fear and went down there again and brought back for her the mirror of my great-grandmother. As she saw it, she laughed with joy, then clutched at it and kissed it, and devoured it with her eyes.

❖ ❖ ❖

More than ten years have passed by since then and still she stares incessantly into the mirror, not turning away an instant.

"Is it really me?" she whispers and her face, as she blushes, shines with serene delight. "Yes, it is! All things tell lies to me except this mirror. People lie, my husband lies. Oh, if only I had seen myself earlier, I would have known what I truly am and would never have married that man! He is quite unworthy of me. The most handsome and noble of knights should be at my feet."

Once, as I stood behind my wife, I glanced inadvertantly into the mirror—and learned a terrible secret. I saw there a woman of such dazzling beauty as I have never seen in all my life, a wonder of nature, a figure of comeliness, grace and love.

How can I explain it? What had happened? Why did my ugly lumbering wife look so lovely in the mirror? Why?

Because, indeed, the distorting mirror distorted every line of my wife's ugly face and by this changing of the features chanced to make it beautiful. A minus times a minus is a plus.

And now both of us, my wife and I, sit at the mirror, not

turning away an instant, looking: my nose twists up my left cheek, my chin is cleft and turned askew but my wife's face is fascinating—and an insane passion overcomes me.

"Ha, ha, ha!"

I laugh savagely. And my wife whispers, scarcely heard.

"How lovely I am!"

1883

HE AND SHE

❖ ❖ ❖

THEY ARE WANDERERS. IT IS ONLY TO PARIS THAT THEY DEVOTE months; as for Berlin, Vienna, Naples, Madrid, St. Petersburg and other cities, they are chary of their time. In Paris they feel, as it were, at home: it is their capital and place of residence. But the rest of Europe is boring and unspeakably provincial, only to be looked at through the lowered shutters of grand hotels or a proscenium arch.

They are not old but they've had time to visit all the big cities of Europe two or three times. By now Europe bores them and they begin to speak of a trip to America; and speak of it they will until such time they cease to be convinced her splendid voice is worth exhibiting in either hemisphere.

It is difficult to see them. In the streets it is impossible because they travel by coach, after dark, in the evenings or at night. They sleep till lunch time; and they wake up usually in a bad mood and receive no one. Only occasionally do they have visitors, by uncertain appointment, backstage, or as they take supper.

You can see her on photographs that are on sale. There she is a beauty, but beautiful she has never been. Don't believe her photographs: she is ugly. Most people see her as they look at a stage. But on stage she is unrecognizable: white lead, rouge, Indian ink and false hair cover her face like a mask. It is the same at concerts.

Playing *Marguerite*, she, twenty-seven, lumpish, wrinkled, her nose covered with freckles, looks like a slender, pretty girl of seventeen. The last person she resembles on stage is herself.

If you want to see them, obtain an invitation to one of the dinners given for her, or sometimes by her, before they leave one city for another. To obtain one is only easy at first sight for only select people secure places at the tables . . . These, by money and connections, are critics, climbers pretending to be critics, singers and conductors who reside there, dilettantes and connoisseurs with sleek bald heads, habitués of opera and sycophants. The dinners are not boring for one who likes to observe interesting people . . . They are worth visiting twice.

These interesting people (and there are many at the dinners) eat and chat. Their postures are most free and easy: neck to one side, head to the other, one elbow on the table. Old men even pick their teeth.

Critics who write in the newspapers are at the tables nearest to hers. Nearly all are drunk and very familiar in their behaviour as if they'd known her for a hundred years. A degree more and they'd be taking liberties. They joke loudly, drink, interrupt one another (not forgetting to say, "Pardon,") propose pompous toasts with no apparent fear of looking foolish; some fall about in gentlemanly fashion across the corner of the table and kiss her hand.

The would-be critics talk didactically to the dilettantes and the connoisseurs; who in their turn say nothing. They envy the critics, smile blissfully and drink to the one and only beauty who is especially beautiful on these occasions.

She, the queen of the occasion, is unpretentiously dressed but at fearful expense. A huge diamond glances from under the lace frills about her neck. On each arm is a bracelet, massive and smooth. Her hair style is remarkably diffuse: pleasing to women, not to men. Her face is radiant, beaming a broad smile at the assembled company. She can smile on all at once,

converse with all at once, graciously nodding her head, a nod
for each one there.

Look at her face and you think that there are only friends
about her for whom she has most friendly feelings. When the
dinner ends, she gives her photograph to someone and writes
on the back of it, there at the table, her autograph and the
name of the fortunate recipient. She makes a speech, of course,
in French and other languages. She speaks English and German
so badly it is laughable but that very badness comes graciously
from her. In fact, she is so gracious you have long ago forgotten
she is ugly.

And he? He, *le mari d'elle*, sits five tables away from her.
He drinks a great deal, eats a great deal, is a long time silent,
rolls his bread into little balls and keeps reading the labels on
the bottles. Looking at his face, you feel he's at a loose end,
lazy, bored, fed-up . . .

He is fair-haired with bald patches in streaks across his
head. Women, wine, sleepless nights and gadding about in high
society have furrowed his face with deep wrinkles. He's thirty-
five, no more, but looks older. It is as if his face has been
soaked in kvass. His eyes are handsome but lazy . . . Once he
wasn't ugly but now he is. His legs are crooked, his hands the
colour of earth and his neck hairy. Because of his bow legs
and most peculiar walk they mock him in Europe as "the
perambulator." In evening dress he's like a wet jackdaw with
a dry tail. The guests take no notice of him. He repays in kind.

Go to one of the dinners and look at them, the pair of them,
observe and tell me then what brought and keeps them together.

You'll watch and answer more or less like this:

"She's a famous singer and he—only the husband of a famous singer, or, as they say backstage, the husband of the
lady. She earns up to eighty thousand a year in Russian money,
he does nothing and so has time to be her servant. She needs
a cashier and a man to deal with managers, contracts and
negotiations . . . She's only concerned with the applause of
audiences, as for bookings and that side of her profession she

does not deign to take an interest, it's not her affair. And so
she needs him, needs him as hanger-on, as servant . . . She'd
get rid of him if she could manage such things herself. He is
even—getting, as he does, a solid stipend (she doesn't know
the value of money)—in league with her lady's maids to cheat
her and, as sure as two times two makes four, squanders her
money, making free quite carelessly with what perhaps she's
put by for a rainy day—and snug in his situation burrows like
a worm in a fine apple. He'd leave her if she hadn't money."

They all think and say that who look at them during the
dinners. They do so because, unable to look into the depth of
the matter, they can only judge by appearances. They gaze on
her, as on a wonder, and avoid him, as if he were a pygmy
covered in frog slime; yet this wonder of Europe is bound to
this frog by an enviable, rare bond.

This is what he writes:

"You ask me why I love this shrew. To tell the truth, the
woman's unworthy of love. And she's unworthy of hatred. She
only deserves a total lack of notice, a disregard of her existence.
In order to love her you have to be me or a madman which,
indeed, amounts to the same thing.

"She is plain. When I married her she was ugly and now she
is worse. She has no forehead. Instead of brows are two scarcely
visible tiny stripes above her eyes, instead of eyes themselves
two shallow chinks. Nothing shines in those chinks: neither
wit, nor longing, nor passion. Her nose, it's a potato. Her
mouth is small and beautiful but her teeth are horrible. She
has no breasts or waist. Though that defect is smoothed over
by the devilishly clever way—like supernatural art—she
clamps herself into a corset. She is short and plump; and her
plumpness goes flabby. *En masse*, through all her body runs a
deformity I count of great importance: a total lack of feminin-
ity. Paleness of skin and weakness of muscle I don't regard as
feminine and in this I differ from many. She's neither ladylike
nor genteel: she's a crude-mannered marketwoman. Walking,
she waves her arms about; sitting, one leg over the other, she

rocks to and fro with all her body; lying down, she sticks her feet up; and so on . . .

"She is slovenly. Her trunks are typical: clean linen mixed up in there with dirty, cuffs with slippers and my boots, new corsets with broken ones. We never receive guests because there's such filthy disorder in our rooms . . . Oh, but what are you to say? See her at midday when she wakes up and creeps out lazily from under her blanket and you wouldn't recognize in her the woman with a voice like a nightingale. Unkempt, with tangled hair and sleepy, puffy eyes, in a nightdress torn at the shoulders, barefoot and scowling in a cloud of last night's tobacco smoke—how is she like a nightingale?

"She drinks: drinks like a trooper whatever and whenever she likes. She's been drinking for a long time. If she didn't drink, she'd have been greater than Patti or at any rate no less. She's drunk away half her career and very soon she'll drink away the other half. German rascals taught her to drink beer and now she doesn't go to bed without drinking last thing two or three bottles. If she didn't drink, she wouldn't have catarrh of the stomach.

"She's uncouth, as the students who sometimes invite her to their concerts will tell you.

"She loves publicity. It costs us some thousand francs a year. I despise it with all my heart. However much this stupid publicity may cost, it will always cheapen her voice. My wife loves flattery but not the truth unless it flatters. To her the bought kiss of Judas is no sweeter than the bought praise of a critic. She has a total lack of self-respect.

"She's clever but her mind is untrained. Her brain has long lost its flexibility: it's muffled in fat and going soft.

"She's capricious, erratic and hasn't a single firm conviction. Yesterday she said that money was trash, that the heart of things was not there, but today she's giving concerts in four places because she's come to the conclusion that there's nothing on this earth of more importance. Tomorrow she'll say what she said yesterday. She has no wish to know her native land. She has no political heroes, no favourite newspapers, no favourite authors.

"She's rich but she does not help the poor. What's more, she doesn't pay her bills to milliners or hairdressers. She's heartless.

"She's a spoilt woman, a thousand times over!

"But watch this shrew as, girded, sleek and ointmented, she moves towards the footlights to rival in song the larks and nightingales who greet the dawn in May. The charm and grace of her swanlike motion! Look, I beg you, pay attention! As she first raises her hand and opens her mouth, those shallow chinks become wide eyes, gleaming with passion. Nowhere else could you find such splendid eyes. When she, my wife, begins to sing, as the first trills ripple into the air and I start to feel my troubled mind grow calm by power of wonderful sound, look then at my face and you will learn the secret of my love.

"I ask my neighbours then: "Isn't she beautiful, really beautiful?"

"Yes," they reply, but it's not enough for me. I would like to annihilate anyone who could dream this splendid woman isn't my wife. I forget everything, all that's past, and live only in that moment.

"See what an artist she is! How deep the meaning of her every movement! Everything is known to her: love and hatred and the human heart . . . It's not for nothing that the theatre thunders with applause.

"When the last scene is over, I take her from the theatre, blanched and exhausted by living through a lifetime in a single evening. I am pale as well, worn out. We sit in the carriage and drive to the hotel. There, quietly, without undressing, she falls on the bed. And I, quietly, sit beside it and kiss her hand. On those evenings she doesn't send me away. We cuddle up together and sleep till morning, and wake to curse each other to the devil . . .

"Do you know when else I love her? When she appears at balls or dinners. It is then I love in her the wonderful actress.

What an artist you have to be to outwit and master her nature as she can. I don't recognize her at those stupid dinners. She has made a peacock out of a plucked goose . . ."

This letter is written in a drunken, scarcely legible script. It is in German and thick with spelling mistakes.

This is what she writes:

"You ask me whether I love this fellow? Yes, sometimes . . . Why? God knows . . .

"It is true he is ugly and unlikable. Men of his sort are not born with a claim on reciprocal love. Men of his sort can only purchase it, it isn't given freely to them. Judge for yourself.

"He is drunk as a cobbler both day and night. His hands shake in a most unpleasant way. When he's drunk, he's grumpy and uncouth. And he beats me. When he's sober, he lies down on no matter what and doesn't say a word.

"He's always threadbare though he's not short of money for clothes. Half my takings slip away I don't know where through his hands.

"I can in no way manage to control him. For unhappily married artistes, expenses are terribly high. The husbands take half the income for their trouble.

"He doesn't squander it on women, I know. He loathes women.

"He's an idler. He sees no need at any time to do any sort of work. He eats, drinks, sleeps—that's all.

"He nowhere completed a course. They expelled him from his first one at university for bad conduct.

"He is not of gentle birth, and, a most awful thing, he's German.

"I am not fond of German gentlemen. In a hundred Germans there are ninety-nine idiots and one genius. And the latter I expect will be a German prince of French extraction.

"He smokes abominable tobacco.

"But he has his good points. More than me he loves my noble art. When before a performance they announce that I cannot sing because I am ill, which is naughty of me, he goes about like someone stunned, clenching his fists.

"He is not a coward or afraid of people. I love him most of all when he is among people. I will tell you a little incident from my life. It happened in Paris a year after I entered the conservatory. I was still very young then and learning how to get drunk. Every evening I was as tipsy as my young resources would allow. I drank, of course, in company. At one of these drinking bouts, as I clinked glasses with my admirers, a very ugly young man whom I did not know came to the table, looked me straight in the eye and asked:

" 'What are you getting drunk for?'

"We burst out laughing. My young man wasn't embarrassed.

"His second question was more impertinent and came straight from the heart:

" 'Why are you laughing? The scoundrels who ply you now with drink won't give you a farthing when you've sung away your voice and become a pauper!'

"How impudent! My companions made a great fuss. But I sat the young man down beside me and ordered wine for him. Apparently this champion of temperance had a lively taste for wine. And by the way I only call him young because his whiskers were so scanty.

"I paid him for his impudence by marrying him.

"He is very quiet. Mostly he speaks only a word or two. He speaks them chestily, a quaver in his throat, taut-faced. It occurs to him to do it as he sits among a group of people at a dinner or a ball . . . If someone (no matter who) tells a lie, he lifts his head and, regardless of everything, quite unembarrassed, says:

" 'That's not true!'

"It's his favourite phrase. What woman could resist his shining eyes as he says it. I love that phrase of his and the flash in his eyes and the taut expression of his face. Not everyone can speak those lovely impudent words and my husband speaks them all the time and everywhere. I love him sometimes and those 'sometimes,' as far as I remember, coincide with him speaking those lovely words.

"But all the same, God knows why I love him. I'm a bad

psychologist and in the event it seems this is a psychological question . . ."

This letter is written in French in an elegant, almost masculine hand. You cannot find in it a single grammatical error.

1882

Two Scandals

❖ ❖ ❖

"Stop, the devil take you! If you goat-voiced tenors can't sing in tune, then I'll clear out! Look at the notes, Ginger! You, Ginger, third on the right! I'm talking to *you*! If you don't know how to sing, why the devil do you come here, cawing like a crow on the stage? Start again!"

He shouted and struck the score with his baton. These long-haired conductors get away with a great deal. It has to be like that. Indeed, if he storms and curses and tears his hair, it's for his sacred art with which no liberties may be taken. He is the watchdog of that art and but for him would not the singers send appalling semi-tones into the air, distorting and destroying harmony? For Harmony he cherishes: in the cause of Harmony he'd end the world or end himself. It won't do to be angry with him. If he were out for his own interests, it would be different.

Most of his bitter reproach and rage he vented on the ginger-haired girl, third in line on the right. He could have torn her apart, trampled her into the ground, knocked her to bits and thrown her out of the window. She sang more out of tune than all of them and he hated and despised her, that ginger-head, more than anything in the world. If she'd fallen through the

floor or died just there before his eyes or if the greasy lamp-
lighter set her burning instead of the lamps or thrashed her on
the spot, he would have laughed for joy.

"Oh, go to the devil! Understand once and for all you know
as much about music and singing as I know about whale-
fishing. I'm talking to you, Ginger! Get it into her head it's
not F Sharp, it's a simple F! Teach the clot her notes! Now,
sing on your own! Begin! Second violin, go like the devil with
your unrosined bow!"

The eighteen-year-old girl stood staring at her score and
trembled like a string plucked violently by fingers. Her little
face kept flaring like a fire; and her eyes glistened with tears
ready to drop any moment on the little black pin-heads of the
music. She'd have been happy if her silky, glistening hair,
tumbling on back and shoulders, could hide her face from
everyone.

Her breast heaved under her bodice like a wave, and beneath
both bodice and breast was fearful ferment: grief, remorse,
panic and self-contempt. The poor girl felt guilty, conscience
pricking everywhere, it seemed, within: guilty before her art,
before the conductor, her colleagues, the orchestra. And indeed she would feel guilty before an audience. If they booed
her off the stage, they'd be right a thousand times over. Her
eyes were afraid of looking at people and she felt they were all
looking at her with hatred and contempt . . . Especially *him*!
He could have thrown her to the other end of the world, as far
away as possible from his musical ears.

"Oh God, make me sing properly!" she thought and in her
violently trembling soprano there sounded a note of despair.
He wouldn't heed that note and he cursed and clutched his
long hair. Suffering didn't matter a damn: there was a performance that evening!

"It's utterly appalling! The wench knifes my guts with her
nanny-goat bleat! You're not a primadonna, you're a washerwoman! . . . Take the music from that Gingerhead! . . ."

She'd have been happy if she could sing well, not out of tune

. . . She knew how to sing properly, she was a skilful performer. Was she really to blame if her eyes wouldn't obey her? Those lovely but disloyal eyes that she'd curse till her dying day, instead of looking at the music and following the movements of the baton, they stared at his hair and into his eyes . . . The tousled hair and eyes that flashed, so terrible to see, were fascinating to her own. The poor girl was head over ears in love with that face of brooding clouds and lightning flashes. Was she to blame if her little mind, instead of concentrating on rehearsal, thought of quite other things that thwarted her work, her life, her peace of mind . . .

Her eyes stared at the notes, moved from the notes to his baton, from his baton to his white tie, his chin, his moustaches and on and on and on . . .

"Take the music from her! She's sick!" he shouted finally. "I can't go on!"

"Yes, I'm sick," she whispered humbly, ready to ask a thousand pardons . . .

They let her go home and her place was taken by another who hadn't as good a voice but could pay attention and work decently and diligently with no thought of white tie or moustaches.

But at home he gave her no peace. When she got there from the theatre, she fell on the bed. She hid her face under the pillow and saw in the dark of her closed eyes his features twisted with rage: he seemed to be beating her about the temples with his baton. This arrogant fellow was the first man she was in love with.

But the web was spoiled before it was spun.

Next day after rehearsal her colleagues came to ask how she was. It was printed in the papers and on the playbills that she was taken ill. The manager came and the producer and each expressed respectful sympathy. And *he* came as well.

When he isn't standing before the orchestra or looking at his score, he's quite a different man. He is courteous then, as friendly and respectful as a young man. A sweet, polite smile

comes on his face. Far from cursing anyone to the devil he's
even afraid of smoking or crossing one leg over the other in
front of ladies. You couldn't find a nicer or more decent fellow.

He came most anxious of face to say her illness was a blow
to art and that all his colleagues and he too would give anything for the health and well-being of *"notre petit rossignol."*
Oh, these illnesses! What damage they do to art! The manager
had to be told that, if the draught still blew across his stage,
no one would work, they'd all leave. Health was more valuable
than anything on earth! He shook her little hand with feeling,
sighed sincerely, asked to be allowed to call again and, cursing
at illness, went away.

A splendid fellow! Nevertheless when she told them she
was well and appeared again upon the stage, he cursed her to
the blackest of black devils and once again the lightning
flashed across his face.

On the whole, though, he's a very decent chap. Once she
was standing in the wings, leaning against a rose bush that
had flowers made of wood, and following his movements with
her eyes. She held her breath in rapture at the sight of him.
He was standing with Mephistopheles and Valentine, drinking
champagne and laughing loudly. Jokes poured from the lips
that often cursed men to the devil.

He drank three glasses, then left the singers and made for
the passage to the orchestra where violinists and cellists were
already tuning up. He went by her, smiling, beaming and ges-
ticulating, his face aglow with satisfaction. Who was there to
say he wasn't a good conductor? No one dared!

She blushed and smiled at him. Tipsy, he stopped beside her
and began to speak:

"I'm so mellow tonight! My God, I feel marvellous! Ha ha!
You're so lovely tonight! You have wonderful hair! My God,
haven't I really noticed till now what a wonderful mane this
nightingale has?"

He stooped and kissed her shoulder that the hair hung down
upon.

"I'm so mellow because of this damned wine . . . My dear

nightingale, we'll not make any more mistakes, will we? And we'll sing with proper care, won't we? Why are you out of tune so often? It didn't use to be like that, my golden head!"

Quite carried away, the conductor kissed her hand. She too began speaking:

"Don't scold me . . . You see I . . . I . . . I . . . You'll kill me with your scolding . . . I can't stand it . . . I beg you! . . ."

And tears welled up in her eyes. Not knowing what she was doing, she leaned against his elbow and almost clung to him.

"You don't know, you see . . . You're so spiteful. I beg you . . ."

He sat down on the bush and almost slid off it. To stop sliding he clutched her round the waist.

"There's the bell, my little one. See you at the next interval!"

After the performance she didn't ride home alone. *He* rode with her, tipsy, laughing with joy, maudlin with sentiment. How happy she was! Oh God! She rode along, feeling him embrace her, unable to believe in her happiness. She felt that fate must be deceiving her!

But be that as it may, for a full week the public read on the posters that the conductor and *that lady of his* were unwell. The girl only let him go when it became awkward hiding away from people and doing no work.

"We'll have to give our love a little air," said the conductor on the seventh day. "I'm pining without my orchestra."

On the eighth day he was already waving his baton and cursing all and sundry, even "Gingerhead."

Women of her kind love like cats. My heroine, having lured her *bête noire* and begun to live with him, didn't give up her foolish habits. As before, instead of the music and his baton, she looked at his tie and his face . . . During rehearsal and performance she still sang out of tune, even worse than before. And he paid her back with abuse. Before, he'd abused her only at rehearsals, now he did it at home afterwards, standing before her bed.

How sentimental she was! It was enough as she sang to look

at his dear face and she'd come in a full beat too late or her voice quiver. She stared at him from the stage as she sang and, when she wasn't singing, she stood in the wings, her eyes never away from his tall figure. During the interval they met in a dressing room, drank champagne together and made fun of her admirers. When the orchestra played the overture, she stood on stage and peeped at him through a little hole in the curtain. Performers used it to snigger at the bald heads in the front row or guess the size of an audience from the number they saw.

This hole in the curtain destroyed her happiness. It caused a scandal.

One Shrovetide—and audiences are fairly good then—they were performing *The Hugenots*. As the conductor moved among the music stands toward his place, she was already at the curtain, watching him, avid and heartsick, through the hole. He made a grave, sour face and waved his baton to this side and to that. The overture began.

At first his handsome face was relatively calm . . . But then, as the central section came nearer, a lightning flicker crossed his right cheek and his eye screwed up. The sounds to his right were ragged, then a flautist played out of tune and a bassoonist coughed at an unfortunate moment, for a cough can delay the entry of a theme. At this his left cheek flashed and twitched. Oh, the spasms and fire of his face! She looked at him and was in seventh heaven, at the height of bliss.

"Curse that cellist!" he muttered through his teeth and it was almost heard.

That cellist knows the notes but rejects the spirit of them! How can you give a tender-sounding instrument like that to people of no feeling? . . . Spasms crossed his face and his free fist clutched the music stand as if the stand itself were guilty, making a fat cellist play only for money, not for contentment of the spirit.

"Get off the stage!" sounded a voice nearby.

The face of the conductor suddenly lightened and beamed with joy. His lips smiled. A difficult passage had been rendered with more than brilliance by the first violins. How that delights a conductor's heart! It delighted the heart too of my ginger-haired heroine as if she played first violin herself and her heart were a conductor's too. But a conductor's it was not, that heart, even if a conductor were the lord of it. His "ginger-headed witch" saw his face smile and smiled herself . . . but it was not the time for smiling. Something weird and awfully silly was happening . . .

The hole suddenly disappeared before her eyes. Where had it gone to? There was a sound of some sort up above as if a steady wind blew. Something was moving slowly up past her face. She began looking for the hole to see his dear face but instead of a hole she suddenly saw a wide mass of light above and below . . . And from it emerged innumerable lamps and heads, and among those heads of various kinds she saw the conductor's. His head looked at her, wonder-struck. Then wonder gave way to indescribable horror and desperation . . .

Without noticing she moved half a step towards the footlights. A laugh sounded from the upper circle and quickly all the theatre was awash with continuous laughter and hissing. What the devil! There, to sing in *The Hugenots*, a lady in gloves, hat and frock of the very latest fashion!

Ha ha ha!

The bald heads of the front row shook with laughter. There was uproar . . . And his face went as old and wrinkled as Aesop's! He breathed hatred and curses . . . He stamped his foot and threw to the ground the baton he wouldn't have changed for a field marshall's. Thereupon the orchestra made a mess of things and went silent . . . She stepped back, staggered and glanced to one side . . . There from the wings stared pale and angry faces . . . Their beastly snouts hissed . . .

"You're ruining us!" hissed the stage manager.

The curtain crept slowly down and waved uncertainly about, as if lowered when it shouldn't be . . . She reeled and clutched the wings for support . . .

"You're ruining me, you shameless idiot! Devil take you, filthy bitch!"

The voice that spoke had whispered to her, preparing for the theatre: "I can't help loving you, my little one. You're my good angel! Your kiss is worth Mahomet's heaven!" But now? She was ruined, no doubt about it, ruined!

When order was restored in the theatre and the furious conductor began the overture a second time, she was already at home. She hurriedly undressed and flung herself under the bedclothes. It isn't as terrible to die lying down as sitting or standing and she was sure remorse and grief would kill her. She hid her head under the pillow and, afraid to think and trembling with shame, she twisted about under the quilt. It smelt of the cigars *he* smoked . . . What would he say when he came?

He came at three o'clock in the morning. He was drunk: had got drunk in grief and fury. His legs were sagging and his hands trembled like leaves in a gentle wind. He pulled off neither his fur coat nor cap, came up to the bed and stood there a minute, silent. She held her breath.

"So you can sleep in peace when you've disgraced yourself in front of everyone!" he hissed. "Oh, a real artist, you know how to keep your conscience quiet! A real artist! Pah! You're a witch!"

He ripped the quilt from her and flung it in the fireplace.

"Know what you've done? You've made a fool of me! I'll have to let you go to the devil! Do you know that? Or don't you? Get up!"

He dragged her up by the hand. She sat on the edge of the bed and hid her face in her tousled hair.

"Forgive me!"

"Pah! Ginger!"

He clutched at her nightdress and saw a lovely shoulder, white as snow. But shoulders were nothing to him now.

"Out of my house! Get dressed! You've poisoned my life, you scum!"

She went to the chair where her clothes lay in a muddled heap and began to dress. She'd poisoned his life! How mean and wicked to poison the life of that great man! She'd go away lest she did more of such wickedness. Then let someone else poison his life . . .

"Out of here! This minute!"

He flung her jacket in her face and gnashed his teeth. She finished dressing and stood by the door. He became silent. But that didn't last very long. Swaying, he pointed to the door. She went out to the landing. He opened the door to the street.

"Get out, slut!"

And grabbing her slender back, he threw her out.

"Goodbye!" she whispered, penitent, and disappeared in darkness.

It was foggy and cold . . . Thin rain was drizzling from the sky . . .

"To the devil with you!" he shouted after her and, deaf to her splashing in the mud, locked the door. Having thrown his girl-friend into the cold fog, he lay down in the warm bed and soon was snoring.

"Serves her right!" he said, as he woke in the morning. But he was deceiving himself! Grief gnawed at his musical heart strings and yearning for his ginger-haired girl tormented his spirit. For a week he went about as if half drunk, grieving, waiting for her return, tormented by lack of news. He thought she would come back, was sure of it . . . But she didn't. Poisoning a man she loved more than life was not in her programme.

They crossed out her name from the list of artists for "improper conduct." They could not forgive the scandal she caused. She wasn't informed of her dismissal because no one knew where she had gone . . . They knew nothing but imagined a great deal . . .

"She's frozen to death or has drowned herself," thought the conductor.

After six months they forgot about her. The conductor forgot. A handsome artist has many women on his conscience and to recall each one is too much for the memory.

All are duly punished in this life. So say the virtuous and devout. Was the conductor?

Yes, he was!

Five years later the conductor was passing through the town of X. It has a splendid operatic company and he stopped a day there to get to know its members. He put up at the best hotel and by morning he received a letter which clearly shows the popularity of my long-haired hero.

It contained an invitation to conduct *Faust*. The conductor N. had been taken suddenly ill, his baton laid down for another's use. Would my hero be prepared, they asked, to take the opportunity and by his art delight the devotees of music in the town of X? My hero consented.

He took up the baton and musicians strange to him now saw the clouds and lightning of his face. A lot of lightning. No wonder! There'd been no time for rehearsal and by his art he had to dazzle there and then at the performance.

The first act went well. And so did the second. But in the third there was a little trouble. Habitually a conductor doesn't look at the stage or anywhere else. All his attention is on the score. So, when in the third act, Marguerite, a splendid, strong-voiced soprano, began to sing at the spinning-wheel, he smiled with pleasure: the lady sang beautifully.

But when this same lady came in late at the eighth bar, the lightning flashed across his face again and he stared with anger at the stage. Checkmate to the lightning! His eyes opened wide in amazement and his eyes went big as a bull-calf's.

On stage, at the spinning wheel, sat the ginger-haired girl he'd driven from a warm bed to thrust into the dark, cold fog. There she sat, at the spinning wheel, but not quite as when he drove her out, different. Her face was as before but not her voice and body. They were more elegant and graceful, flexible and assured.

The conductor gaped and went pale. His baton gave a nervous jerk, dithered in confusion about one spot, then froze.

"It's her!" he said aloud and laughed.

Surprise, delight and rapture without measure overwhelmed him. The ginger-head whom he had driven out had not died but become magnificent. It delighted his maestro's heart. Another star of music: the artist in him was transported!

"It's her! Her!"

His baton froze and, when he moved it again to get things going, it fell from his hand and hit the floor. The first violin stared at him in surprise and bent down to pick up the baton. The cellist thought the conductor was ill, stopped playing, then started again, but in the wrong place. Sounds spun and twisted in the air and, seeking to right themselves, crashed together in a fearful jangle . . .

She, his ginger-headed Marguerite, jumped up and stared with anger at "those drunkards who . . ."

She went pale and her eyes looked the conductor up and down.

And the audience, caring only for their money's worth, began to mutter and whistle . . .

Marguerite, to crown it all, screamed right across the theatre and, lifting up her hands, lurched at full height toward the footlights. She had recognized him and now saw nothing but the clouds and lightning of his face.

"Oh, the damned slut!" he shouted and struck the score with his fist.

What would Gounod have said when such mockery was made of his creation? Oh, Gounod would have killed him, and rightly so!

He had blundered for the first time in his life and for that blunder, that disgrace, he'd not forgive himself.

He ran out of the theatre, blood on his lower lip, ran to his hotel and locked himself in his room. He stayed locked in three days and nights, preoccupied, it seemed, in self-analysis, self-torture.

The players say he went grey-haired in those three days and tore half the hair from his head . . .

"I've treated her shamefully!" he weeps as he drinks. "I've ruined her in her role! I'm . . . not a conductor!"

But why did he say nothing of that when he threw her out?

1882

A WOMAN WITHOUT PREJUDICES
A ROMANCE

❖ ❖ ❖

MAXIM KUZMICH SALUTOV IS BIG, BROAD-SHOULDERED AND portly. His physique is certainly athletic and his strength is extraordinary. He can bend a twenty copeck piece, uproot a young tree, lift a weight with his teeth and he swears that no man in the world dare wrestle with him. He is brave and bold. Other people, though, go pale and tremble when he's angry. Men and women yelp and redden when he shakes their hand: it hurts. It is impossible to listen to his splendid baritone for it is deafening. A strong man indeed. I know no other like him.

But this monstrous, superhuman, oxlike strength became as nothing, as a mere squashed rat, when Maxim Kuzmich told Elena Gavrilovna that he loved her. He blenched, blushed, trembled and hadn't the strength to lift a chair as he forced from his big mouth the words: "I love you." His strength withdrew, leaving his great body a huge empty vessel.

He told her of his love on the skating rink. She fluttered light as a feather over the ice and he came after her, trembling, agitated and muttering. Suffering was written on his face . . .

His agile, nimble legs gave way and tangled up as he tried to cut an intricate pattern on the ice . . . Afraid of a rebuff, you'd think? Oh no. Elena Gavrilovna loved him and longed for him to offer her his hand and heart . . . She, a petite, attractive brunette was likely any moment to burn away with sheer impatience . . . He was thirty already, of minor rank, a low grade official with little money, but then he was so handsome, so nimble-witted and so agile. He danced beautifully, was a magnificent shot, and no one could ride like him. Once, when she was with him, he cleared a ditch at which a splendid English jumper would have hesitated.

Impossible not to love a man like that!

And he himself knew that she loved him. He was certain of it. But one thought made him suffer . . . It stifled his mind, made him fume and weep, and would not let him drink or eat or sleep . . . It poisoned his life. He vowed his love and yet it seethed in his brain and beat at his temples.

"Be my wife!" he told Elena Gavrilovna. "I love you! Madly! Terribly!"

But at that very time he thought:

"Have I the right to be her husband? No, I haven't! If she knew my origins, if somebody told her about my past, she'd box my ears. My unworthy, miserable past! She's distinguished, rich, accomplished, she'd spurn me if she knew me for the bird I am!"

When Elena Gavrilovna flung herself about his neck and vowed her love, it didn't make him happy.

That thought poisoned everything . . . Going home from the skating rink, he bit his lips and pondered:

"I'm a scoundrel! If I were an honourable man, I'd have told her everything . . . everything! Before I told her that I loved her, I should have let her know my secret! But I didn't do it, I'm a villain, a scoundrel!"

Elena's parents agreed to her marriage with Maxim Kuzmich. They liked the athlete: he was deferential and as a civil servant had considerable hope of advancement. Elena

Gavrilovna was in the clouds, most happy. But the poor athlete was far from happy. Until the very wedding the thought tormented him that one day he would have to tell . . .

And a friend tormented him too, a friend who knew his past like the palm of his hand . . . He had to give him nearly all his salary.

"Invite me to dinner at the Hermitage!" said the friend. "Or I'll tell everybody . . . And lend me twenty-five roubles!"

Poor Maxim Kuzmich crumpled and shrunk. His cheeks sagged, his fists became veined and sinewy. The thought made him ill. But for the woman he loved he would have shot himself . . .

"I'm a villain, a scoundrel!" he thought. "I must tell her before the wedding! Let her spurn me!"

But he didn't tell her before the wedding: he hadn't the courage.

And the thought that, after he told her, he would have to leave the woman he loved, was more terrible still.

The wedding day came. They crowned the young couple, drank their health and expressed astonishment at their happiness. Poor Maxim Kuzmich replied to the toasts, drank, danced, laughed, but was fearfully unhappy.

"Brute that I am, I'll force myself to tell her! They have crowned us in marriage but it's still not too late. We can separate!"

And tell her he did!

When the longed-for hour came and the young couple were escorted to the bedroom, conscience and honour took their course . . . Maxim Kuzmich, pale, trembling, forgetting their close relationship, scarcely breathing, timidly went to her, took her hand and said:

"Before we can be united . . . one with another . . . I have to . . . I have to . . . explain . . ."

"What's the matter, Max? You're . . . pale! All day you've been pale and silent . . . Are you ill?"

"I . . . I must tell you everything . . . Dearest . . . Let's sit down . . . I have to hurt you, mar your happiness . . . but what am I to do? Duty comes first . . . I will tell you about my past . . . Dearest Lelia . . ."

Lelia's eyes widened and she grinned.

"Well, tell me then . . . But be quick, please . . . And don't tremble so."

"I . . . I was born in Tam . . . in Tambov . . . My parents were people of no importance and terribly poor . . . I'll tell you what sort of fellow I was. You'll be horrified . . . Wait. You'll see . . . I was a beggar . . . As a boy I sold apples . . . pears . . ."

"You!"

"Are you horrified? But, my dear, that's not the worst of it. Oh, how miserable I am! You'll curse me, when you know."

"But what is it, then?"

"At twenty . . . I was . . . was . . . Forgive me . . . Don't turn me out! I was . . . was . . . a clown in a circus!"

"You? A clown?"

Salutov, expecting her to slap him, covered his white face with his hands . . . He was near to fainting . . .

"You? A clown?"

And Lelia tumbled off the couch, jumped up and ran forward . . .

What was she doing? She clutched her belly . . . She dashed about the bedroom, and her laughter, as in hysteria, came thick and fast . . .

"Ha ha ha! . . . You were a clown? You? Maxinka . . . Darling! . . . Show me something! Prove you were! . . . Ha ha ha! Go on, darling!"

She rushed to Salutov and embraced him in a big hug.

"Show me something, dear! . . . You darling!"

"Do you know what you're doing? Aren't you unhappy? Don't you despise me?"

"Do something! Can you walk the tightrope? Go on!"

She covered her husband's face with kisses, fawned about him, cuddled up to him. Not a sign that she was angry. Bewildered but delighted, he did what she asked.

Going to the bed, he counted three, then rested his forehead on the edge and put his legs up in the air.

"Bravo, Max! Encore! Ha ha! You darling! Do it again!"

Max swayed, jumped, as it were, to the floor and walked on his hands . . .

In the morning Lelia's parents were terribly surprised.

"Who's that knocking up there?" they asked each other. "The young people are still asleep . . . The servants must be up to their tricks . . . The row they're making! The rascals!"

Father went upstairs but did not find the servants there.

The noise, to his great surprise, was coming from the bedroom of the newly-weds . . . He stood by the door, then shrugged his shoulders and lightly opened it . . . Glancing into the bedroom, he shrivelled up and almost died of astonishment: there, in the middle of the bedroom, Maxim Kuzmich was making a desperate *leap of death* into the air, and Lelia stood applauding. Both faces shone with joy.

1883

HE UNDERSTOOD

❖ ❖ ❖

A STIFLING MORNING IN JUNE. HEAT HANGS IN THE AIR, CRIN-kling up leaves and cracking the surface of the earth. A melan-choly sense of impending thunder. A longing for nature to purge her gloom in rain.

In the west the sky is deep blue with dark furrows. A storm is likely. It will be welcome.

A little stooping man creeps along the edge of the wood. He is about four feet high and is wearing blue trousers with white stripes and huge greyish-brown boots. The tops of them flop halfway down. His trousers, almost impossibly threadbare and patched, hang baggy at the knees and dangle at the back like a coat-tail. His greasy rope-belt has slipped from his belly to his hips and his shirt is working up to his shoulder blades . . .

He carries a shotgun: a rusty barrel about two feet long, its sight like a shoenail, stuck into a homemade butt cut skilfully in white spruce wood with carvings on it, grooves and pat-terns. Without the butt it wouldn't look like a gun at all and with it is like something not of our time . . . medieval . . . The cocking piece, brown with rust, is bound by cord and wire. But the strangest of all is a white gleaming ramrod—just

slashed from a willow—damp and fresh and much too long
for the barrel.

The little man is white-faced. His squinty, inflamed little
eyes glance restlessly up or to the side. His scanty goat-beard
quivers like a rag from his trembling bottom lip. He takes
long, stooping strides and is clearly in a hurry. Behind him,
long tongue hanging grey with dust, runs a big, shaggy mongrel, emaciated as a skeleton dog. From its sides and tail hang
big clusters of old mangy hair. One back leg is bandaged with
a rag and obviously hurts.

The little man keeps glancing back at his companion.

"Back!" he says in a frightened voice.

The mongrel canters back, glances round, waits a moment,
then once more stalks after its master.

The hunter would like to dart off into the wood but it's
impossible: along a wall's edge stretches a thick, prickly black-
thorn and behind it are high, choking weeds and stinging net-
tles . . . Then at last there's a path. The little man gestures
again to his dog, then hurries along the path through bushes.
The earth soughs under his feet: it's not dry yet. It smells
damp, less stifling. Junipers are among the bushes; the real
wood is further on, about three hundred paces.

From the side comes a sound like a squeaky wheel. The
little man quivers and peers into an alder tree. There he notices
a black speck moving, goes nearer and recognizes a young
starling. It is perched on a branch and looking under its lifted
wing. The little man stamps, flings down his cap, presses the
butt to his shoulder and takes aim. This done, he lifts the
cocking piece and holds it lest it fall too soon. The spring and
trigger don't work properly so that it's faulty.

The starling lowers its wing and glances suspiciously at the
hunter. Another second and he'll fly away . . . The little man
takes aim again and lets the cocking piece go. Held too long,
it doesn't fall. The little man tears a cord with his fingernail,
presses a wire and knocks the cocking piece. A rattle, then a
shot. The gun recoils powerfully on the little man's shoulder.
Clearly he's used a lot of powder . . .

He flings down the gun, runs to the alder tree and rummages in the grass. By rotten, mildewed twigs is a little bloodstained patch: he rummages further and finds his victim, a tiny dead thing, still warm, by the tree trunk.

"Got him in the head!" he mutters to the mongrel with delight.

The mongrel sniffs the starling and sees that his master hit her in more places than the head: a gash in her breast, one leg broken, a big drop of blood hanging from her bill . . . The little man feels in his pocket for a new cartridge, and rags, paper and thread spill out. He loads his gun and, eager for more, moves forward . . .

As if out of the earth before him, Krijevetski, the Polish steward, rises up. At the sight of his proud, stern face and red hair the little man goes cold with fear. Of itself his cap falls off.

"What you up to? Shooting?" jeers the Pole. "Very nice!"

The little man glances timidly aside and sees a cart and men beside it. Intent on hunting, he hadn't noticed.

"How dare you shoot here?" asks Krijevetski, louder. "Is this your wood, then? Or do you think it's Peter's day already, open season? Who are you?"

"Pavel Khromoi," says the little man, clutching his gun, scarcely managing to speak. "From Kashilovka."

"From Kashilovka, damn you! Who gave you permission to shoot here?" goes on the Pole, trying not to stress the next to last syllable. "Give me your gun!"

Khromoi gives him the gun and thinks: "Better he sloshed me in the chops than take me in . . ."

"And your cap!"

Khromoi gives him the cap.

"I'll show you how to shoot, curse you! Come on!"

Krijevetski turns his back and walks after the creaking cart. Pavel Khromoi, feeling in his pocket at the starling, follows him . . .

An hour later Krijevetski and Khromoi come into a wide room with a low ceiling and walls of faded blue. The manor

office: no one there but the smell of life about it. In the middle
a big oak table with a couple of ledgers, inkwell and sandbox,
and a teapot with broken spout. All covered with a grey layer
of dust. In one corner a big cupboard, from which paint has
long since peeled, with a kerosene tin on it and a bottle of
some sort of mixture. In the other a little ikon covered by a
spider's web.

"Have to draw up a charge," says Krijevetski. "I'll go tell
the master and fetch a Policeman. Take your boots off!"

Khromoi sits on the floor and quietly, hands trembling,
drags off his boots.

"You won't get away," mutters the steward with a yawn.
"Go off barefoot, be the worse for you! Sit here and wait for
the Policeman . . ."

The Pole locks the boots and the gun in the cupboard and
goes out.

For a long time Khromoi slowly scratches the narrow back
of his head as if wondering where he is. He sighs and looks
about in fear. Cupboard, table, spoutless teapot and ikon look
back at him reproachfully, sadly . . . Flies—the sort that infest
offices—buzz about his head so querulously it makes him feel
terrible . . .

"Zzzz . . ." drone the flies. "Caught, are you? Caught?"

A big bee crawls along the window pane. It's trying to get
out into the air but can't find an opening. Its movements are
very lethargic, miserable . . . Khromoi moves backward to the
door, stops there, runs his hand through his hair and starts to
think . . .

An hour passes, two, and still he waits there, wondering.

His eyes squint at the bee.

"Why doesn't it fly out of the door, the fool?" he asks himself.

Two more hours pass. All around it is still, noiseless, dead . . .

Khromoi begins to think they have forgotten him, that he
won't get away any quicker than the bee that keeps falling
down from the window. When night comes, it will go to sleep.
But what about him?

"People are the same," reasons Khromoi, looking at the bee. "Yes . . . So it is with a man. There's a place where he can get away and be free, but he's too stupid to know where it is, that place . . ."

At last a door slams somewhere. He hears someone's hurrying steps and into the office a minute later comes a little fat man in wide trousers with braces. He has neither coat nor waistcoat. A stripe of sweat lies across his shoulder blades, another across his chest. It is the landowner himself, Pyotr Yegoritch Volchkov, retired lieutenant colonel. His damp brow and fat red face make clear how much he would prefer a crackling frost to the present heat. The closeness oppresses him. His eyes, puffy with sleep, show he has come straight from a soft and stifling bed.

At first he walks a few times up and down, as if he has not noticed Khromoi, then stops in front of him and looks a long time intently into his face, staring with a contempt, first scarcely perceptible in the eyes, then spreading gradually to all his greasy face. Khromoi cannot bear it and lowers his eyes, ashamed . . .

"Show me, yes, show me what you killed!" whispers Volchkov. "Come on, show me, you rascal, William Tell! Show me, you ugly image!"

Khromoi feels in his pocket and brings out the wretched starling. Already the birdlike shape is gone: it has crumpled up and is beginning to wither. Volchkov laughs with scorn and shrugs.

"Fool!" he says. "You perfect fool and empty-headed idiot! Don't you know you've done wrong? Aren't you ashamed?"

"Yes, I am ashamed, Pyotr Yegoritch, sir . . . !" replies Khromoi, struggling against a swallowing that blocks his speech.

"Not only do you come shooting in my forest without permission, you thieving rascal, you're breaking the law of the land! Don't you know there's a law against hunting out of season? No one is allowed to shoot before Peter's day. Don't you know that? Come here!"

Volchkov goes to the table; and Khromoi follows him there.

The landowner opens a book, turns pages for a while, then reads in high-pitched voice the law forbidding hunting before Peter's day.

"Don't you know?" he asks, as he finishes.

"How can't we know? We know, your honour. And we understand it. We know what it's about, don't we?"

"Eh? How can you understand it if you thoughtlessly destroy one of God's creatures? You killed this little bird. What for? Can you bring it back to life? Can you, I say?"

"No, I can't, sir!"

"But you killed it . . . And what use it is to you I do not understand! A starling! Neither flesh nor fowl . . . But you took it upon yourself to kill it . . ."

Volchkov screws up his eyes and tries to straighten out the starling's broken leg. It snaps off and falls on Khromoi's bare foot.

"You're loathsome, loathsome!" goes on Volchkov. "A gobbling plunderer! You did it out of greed! You see a little bird and get angry to see it flying as it likes, praise God . . . "Well, then, I'll kill it . . . and gobble it up!" The greed of men! I can't look at you! Don't stare at me with those eyes of yours! You squint, you squinting rogue! You killed her and perhaps she has little ones . . . Cheeping and cheeping for her now . . ."

Volchkov, making a sad face, lowers his hand to the floor to show how small the little ones might be . . .

"But I didn't do it out of greed, Pyotr Yegoritch," pleads Khromoi with quivering voice.

"Out of what, then? Of course it was greed!"

"No, it wasn't, Pyotr Yegoritch . . . If I took that sin upon me, it wasn't out of greed . . . nor selfishness, Pyotr Yegoritch! The devil worked on me . . ."

"Who are you for the devil to work on! You could work on him! Your sort are crafty thieves, the lot of you!"

Volchkov blows a jet of air from his lungs, draws in some more, then speaks again, less loudly:

"Well, what are we going to do with you? Eh? Taking your crass stupidity into account, we ought to let you go. But considering what you've done and your brazen behaviour, we ought to give you what for ... Not a doubt of it ... That's enough of humoring you ... Enough! I've sent for the Policeman. We'll do what the law requires ... I've sent for him ... The evidence is plain ... You've only yourself to blame ... I'm not punishing you, your sin is ... You knew how to sin, know how to take your punishment. Oh ho! God forgive us sinners. We are wretched ... Well, what sort of crop did you get?"

"Nothing ... sir ..."

"Why are you blinking your eye?"

Embarrassed, Khromoi coughs into his fist and pulls his belt straight.

"Why are you blinking?" repeats Volchkov. "You killed the starling, now you start to cry."

"Your honour," says Khromoi in a rattling falsetto, loud, as if gathering his strength, ". . . it hurts you, in your kindness, that I killed, you see, the little bird. You tell me off, yes, and not because you're the landowner but because it hurts you ... You're human ... But doesn't it hurt me? I'm a stupid chap, without much understanding ... but it hurts me too ... God be my judge!"

"Then why did you shoot it if it hurts you?"

"The devil worked on me. Let me tell you about it, Pyotr Yegoritch ... I'll speak the honest truth as before God ... Let the Policeman come ... It's my sin and I'm to blame, before God and the law ... but I'll tell you the downright truth ... from my heart ... Let me, your honour!"

"Why should I let you or not let you, you're not talking sense? What's it to me? But I won't stand in the way ... Speak! ... Why are you silent? Come on, speak, William Tell!"

Khromoi puts his hand to his quivering lips. His eyes narrow, squint more.

"That starling's nothing to me," he says. "Let them be, starlings and such, what's the use of them? Can't sell them or eat them, they're ... just nothing. You know that yourself ..."

"No, stop that! You a hunter and you don't understand? Starling, if it's roasted, goes well in a stew . . . And with sauce. Like grouse, it's practically the same . . ."

And, as if realising his tone has become matter of fact, Volchkov frowns and says:

"You can find out the taste right now . . . See . . ."

"I'm not talking about the taste . . . It could be bread, Pyotr Yegoritch . . . we know . . . But I killed the starling out of sadness . . . Sadness made me do it . . ."

"What do you mean, sadness?"

"The devil knows what I mean! Let me tell you about it . . . It began to hurt me right from Easter, that sadness . . . Let me tell you about it . . . I walked out, you see, Easter morning, after matins, walked by myself . . . The women were in front and I behind them . . . I walked and walked and stopped by the weir . . . There I stand and look at God's world, and all that's happening in it, see how every creature, every blade of grass, you might say, knows its place . . . It's daybreak and the sun coming up . . . I see it all and I'm glad and I look at the little birds, Pyotr Yegoritch. Suddenly down in my heart somewhere, oh! It must have missed a beat . . ."

"Whatever for?"

"Because I saw the little birds. There and then a thought came in my head . . . How lovely, I think, it'd be to shoot, pity it's against the law . . . And just then two woodcook flew over me in the sky and a snipe called from somewhere over the river. Oh, how I wanted to go hunting! I went home with such imaginings . . . I sit down there, talk with the women, but those same little birds are in front of my eyes. I eat and I hear how the forest stirs and a little bird goes, 'Chirrup, chirrup!' Oh, my God! I want to go hunting and have done with it! . . . The more I drank at my breakfast, the crazier I got! I began to hear a voice. I heard it, a sort of thin, fine voice, an angel's you'd think, ringing in my ears and telling me: 'Go on, Pavel, shoot!' Devil's magic! Your honour, Pyotr Yegoritch, I can testify it was the devil himself and no other. And so sweet and so fine like a child's . . . From that morning it got me, this same yearning sadness . . . I sit there, as it calls, long-faced, like a villain, and I think to myself . . . I think and think . . . And all the time your dead brother's in my mind. Sergei, I mean, heaven be his! I remember, stupid fool that I am, how I went hunting with him, your dead brother. I used to go with his honour, God protect him, as one of his best shots. He noticed and was pleased that I, squinting in both eyes, could shoot like an artist. He wanted to take me to the town to show the doctors the skill I had even though I was so ugly. It was surprising and moving, Pyotr Yegoritch. We used to set off when it was scarcely light, calling our dogs, Kara and Ledka, and . . . oh! We went thirty versts a day! What else can I say? He was like a noble father to me! Pyotr Yegoritch, I tell you truth, but for your brother there never was a real man on this earth. He was cruel, awful, stubborn, but no one could touch him when it came to shooting. His excellency Count Tirbork tried and tried to hunt like him and died of envy. What could he do? He hadn't the style and he couldn't hold a rifle like your brother. Double-barrelled, you know, made by Lepel and Company. A duck! At two hundred paces! Bang! No joking!"

Khromoi quickly wiped his lips, blinked his squinty eyes and went on:

"It was that gave me this yearning sadness. Not to be able to shoot, the misery of it: it chokes my heart!"

"Impudence!"

"No, not at all, Pyotr Yegoritch! All Easter Week I went about like a crazy man. I didn't drink, didn't eat. On Fomin's Day I cleaned my rifle, repaired it . . . I felt better. But on St. George's Day I was sick with the sadness again. It tugged and tugged at me to go hunting and I couldn't stop it for the life of me . . . To go off and drink vodka doesn't help, it makes things worse . . . I'm not being impudent! I got drunk after the Feast of St. Mark . . . and in the morning my sadness was worse than ever . . . It drove me out of my cottage. Oh, how it drove me and drove me! The strength of it! I got my rifle, took it into the kitchen garden and let fly at the jackdaws . . . I hit ten but felt no better: the sadness was driving me to the forest

... to the marshes. And my old woman began to cry shame on me: 'Doesn't do to shoot jackdaws. They're birds of ill omen. It's a sin before God. The crops will fail if you kill them.' I took my rifle, Pyotr Yegoritch, and I smashed it ... The hell with it! I felt relieved ..."

"Impudence!"

"No, not impudence! I tell you truly, Pyotr Yegoritch, I'm not being impudent! Let me tell you about it ... I wake up in the night. I lie there and think ... My old woman's asleep with not a word to say to me ... 'But can I mend my rifle,' I think, 'or can't I?' I get up and go off and mend it."

"Well?"

"Well, nothing ... I mended it and ran out with it like a madman. I was driven on ... There was the path ... I wanted to get a bird right in the snout ... to know about it ..."

"The Policeman's coming ... Go into the passage!"

"I'll go ... And for the heart of me I'm sorry ... Father Pyotr, the priest, he said it was impudence too ... But in my stupid way of understanding things, it isn't impudence, it's illness ... It's like getting drunk ... The same stupid business ... You don't want to do it but it drags at your very soul. You'd be happy not to get drunk. You swear you won't before the ikon, but the longing gets worse and worse ... 'Go on! Drink! Drink!' I know. I've been a drunkard ..."

Volchkov's red nose turns crimson.

"Getting drunk ... That's another matter ..." he says.

"No, they're one and the same, God strike me, one and the same! I tell you true ..."

A silence falls ... For five silent minutes they look at one another.

Volchkov's crimson nose turns purple.

"In fact, it is getting drunk ... Please understand, in your humanity, what a weakness it is."

But the colonel understands not from his humanity but from his own experience.

"Get out!" he says to Khromoi.

Khromoi doesn't understand.

"Get out and don't land yourself here again!"

"My boots, if you please . . ." says the little man, under-standing now and plaintive.

"Well, where are they?"

"In the wardrobe . . ."

Khromoi gets his boots, his cap and his gun. Light of heart he goes out of the office and squints up into the sky at a heavy, black cloud. The first drops are pattering already on the burning roof and all about, in stifling air, oppression lifts.

Volchkov pushes the window from inside. It opens noisily and Khromoi sees the bee fly out.

Air! Khromoi and the bee rejoice in freedom.

1883

75,000

❖ ❖ ❖

Two friends were walking at midnight along Tverskoi Boulevard: one, tall, dark-haired and handsome in threadbare coat of bear's fur and top hat, the other, small and ginger-haired in chestnut overcoat with white bone buttons. Both walked without speaking. The dark-haired man whistled a soft mazurka and the ginger-haired man looked sullenly towards his feet and kept spitting to the side.

"Shall we sit down?" the dark-haired man finally suggested, as they saw the sombre silhouette of Pushkin and the little lamp over the gates of the Monastery of the Passion.

The ginger-haired man agreed without a word and the friends sat down.

"I've a small request to ask of you, Nikolai Borisitch," said the dark man after a certain silence. "Could you lend me ten or fifteen roubles, my friend? In a week's time I'll pay you back . . ."

The ginger-haired man did not speak.

"I wouldn't trouble you if it wasn't necessary . . . Fate played a dirty trick on me today . . . My wife gave me her bracelet to pawn. She has to pay the high school fees for her little sister

. . . I pawned it, you see, and then, there you are . . . I unexpectedly lost at the tables . . ."

The ginger-haired man stirred and grunted.

"You're a shallow man, Vassili Ivanitch!" he said, twisting his mouth in a malicious smile. "A shallow man! What right had you to sit with gentlemen and gamble when you knew it wasn't your money but someone else's? Aren't you a worthless fellow, eh, an empty fop? Wait, don't interrupt . . . Listen, I'll tell you to your face, once and for all . . . Why these perpetual new suits, that pin there in your tie? Have you no idea of what's fitting? Why that stupid top hat? You're living on your wife, yet you pay fifteen roubles for a hat when, with no loss of style or fashion, you could wear one costing three! Why this constant boasting of non-existent friendships with important people? With Khoklov and Plevako and all those editors! When you were telling lies about them today, my eyes and ears burned for you! You tell lies without a blush! And when you were gambling with those gentlemen, losing your wife's money to them, you kept on giving such a stupid smile . . . it was utterly pitiful!"

"Oh, let it drop, let it drop . . . You're in a bad mood today . . ."

"All right, let's say these airs of yours are boyish, adolescent . . . I admit you're still young, Vassili Ivanitch . . . But I won't tolerate . . . There's one thing I can't condone . . . When you were gambling with those fops, how could you be so mean and deceitful? I saw that, when you were dealing, you slipped yourself the ace of spades from under the pack!"

Vassili Ivanitch flushed like a schoolboy and began protesting but the ginger-haired man held his ground. They argued loud and long. Then gradually both quietened and brooded.

"It's true, I completely lost my head," said the dark-haired man after long silence. "It's true . . . I spent all my money, I got into debt, I squandered what belongs to someone else and now I don't know how I'll get out of it. Do you know that awful, unbearable feeling when all your body seems scaly and you've no way of escaping its irritation? I feel something like that now, clustering up to my very ears . . . I'm ashamed of myself in front of people . . . I do a lot of filthy, stupid things for the most trivial reasons, and yet I can't stop doing them . . . It's awful! If I had a legacy or won some money, I'd throw off everything, I think, and be born again . . . But don't you condemn me, Nikolai Borisitch, don't throw stones! Remember the palmist Nekloujev . . ."

"I remember your Nekloujev," said the ginger-haired man. "I remember . . . He squandered other people's money, threw it away, and when the party was over, he wanted to change his ways: he whimpered at the feet of a girl. Before the party, though, he didn't weep . . . It's disgraceful of a writer to make heroes of people who behave like scoundrels. Without his gay, smart look and charming manners the merchant's daughter would not have fallen for this Nekloujev, and there'd have been no repentance. Fate usually gives a smart look to the rogues . . . You're all Don Juans . . . Girls are taken by you, fall in love . . . You're terribly attractive to women!"

The ginger-haired man stood up and walked about near the bench.

"Your wife, for example . . . An honourable and noble woman . . . What reason has she to love you? What reason? And today, yes, all this evening, when you were putting on airs, showing off, just then, an attractive blonde couldn't keep her eyes off you . . . They love you Nekloujevs, they sacrifice themselves to you . . . and yet all your life you beat about and flounder like a fish among the ice . . . Oh, in the name of honesty itself, if only there were a single happy minute! . . . And there's another thing . . . Remember? I was engaged to Olga Alexeevna, your wife, before she knew you. I was quite happy, but then you turned up and I was done for . . ."

"J-j-jealousy!"—the dark-haired man grinned—"I didn't know you were so jealous!"

A look of indignation and disgust passed over the other man's face . . . Mechanically, not realising it himself, he stretched out his hand . . . and swung it. The sound of a blow disturbed the silence of the night . . . The top hat flew from the dark-haired man's head and rolled over the trampled snow. It all happened in a second, quite unexpectedly, and seemed stupid, absurd . . . At once the ginger-haired man was ashamed of that blow. He buried his face in the discoloured collar of his overcoat and began to walk along the boulevard. Reaching Pushkin's statue, he looked round at the dark-haired man, stood a moment without moving and then, as if afraid of something, hurried away . . .

For a long time Vassili Ivanitch sat silent and still. A woman came up to him, laughed and gave him his top hat. He thanked her mechanically, got up and went away . . .

"Now the nagging starts," he thought, as, half an hour later, he climbed the long staircase to his flat. "I'll catch it from the wife for gambling away her money . . . There'll be an all-night sermon! Oh, the devil take her altogether! I'll say I lost the money . . ."

He reached his door and timidly rang. The cook let him in . . .

"Congratulations!" she said, grinning all over her face.

"What for?"

"Oh, you'll see! God took pity!"

Vassili Ivanitch shrugged his shoulders and went into the bedroom. There his wife sat at a table, Olga Alexeevna, a little blonde with curl-papers in her hair. She was writing. In front of her lay some letters already stamped. Seeing her husband, she jumped up and flung her arms about his neck.

"You're here," she said. "What a piece of luck! You can't imagine what a piece of luck! I nearly went hysterical, Vasha, at such a surprise . . . Well, read this!"

And she bounded back to the table, took up a newspaper and put it in front of his face.

"Read it! My ticket has won 75,000. It really is my ticket! Word of honour, it is! I hid it from you because . . . because you would have taken it. When Nikolai Borisitch was engaged to me, he gave me that ticket, and then he didn't want to take it back. What a nice man he is! Now we're terribly rich! You'll turn over a new leaf now, won't live a slovenly life. You see, you cracked up and deceived me out of poverty, living from hand to mouth. I understand. You're intelligent and decent . . ."

Olga Alexeevna walked up and down the room and laughed.

"What a surprise! I was walking and walking, from one corner of the room to the other, cursing you for your dissolute ways, hating you, and then in misery I sat down and read the paper . . . And suddenly I saw it! . . . I've written letters to them all . . . to my sisters, my mother . . . They'll be so pleased, poor things! But where are you going now?"

Vassili Ivanitch looked at the newspaper. Stunned and pale, not listening to his wife, he stood a short time silent, preoccupied, then put on his hat and left the house.

"To Dimitrovka, number N.N.!" he shouted to the coachman.

He didn't find the person he was looking for. Her flat was locked.

"She must be at the theatre," he thought, "or she's dining out after the theatre . . . I'll wait a while . . ."

And wait he did. Half an hour passed, an hour. He walked along the corridor and spoke to a sleepy servant. Below, a clock struck three . . . Finally, losing patience, he went slowly downstairs and out . . .

But fate took pity on him . . .

Just at the door he met a tall, gaunt brunette, a long fur wrap about her neck. About five paces behind followed a man in dark blue spectacles and lambskin hat.

"Excuse me," said Vassili Ivanitch to the lady, "may I disturb you for a minute?"

The lady and the man frowned.

"I'll soon be with you," said the lady to the man and went with Vassili Ivanitch towards a gas bracket. "What do you want?"

"I came to you . . . Nadin . . . about a certain matter . . ." began Vassili Ivanitch, stuttering. "A pity you're with this man or I'd tell you everything . . ."

"But what about? I've no time!"

"You've taken up with new admirers and you've no time! Very well, there's nothing to be said! Why did you break with me on Christmas Eve? You didn't want to live with me because I hadn't the means to provide you with the life you wanted . . . It seems you were wrong. Yes . . . Do you remember that lottery ticket I gave you on your birthday? Well, read this! It's won 75,000!"

The lady took the newspaper and with avid, almost frightened eyes began searching for the Petersburg results . . . And she found . . .

At the very same time other eyes, weeping in dull grief, were looking into a box and searching for a ticket. Those eyes searched all the night but did not find. The ticket had been stolen and Olga Alexeevna knew by whom.

And that same night the ginger-haired man Nikolai Borisitch tossed from side to side, trying to sleep, but could not till the morning. He was ashamed of striking Vassili Ivanitch.

1884

TEARS THE WORLD DOES NOT SEE

❖ ❖ ❖

"Now, NOBLE GENTLEMEN, IT WOULDN'T BE A BAD IDEA TO
have a little supper," said Lieutenant Colonel Rebrotyesov,
garrison commander, tall and thin as a telegraph pole, as he
came out of the club with his friends one dark August night.
"In first rate cities, like Saratov, say, you can always have
supper in the club, but in this stinking Chervyanska of ours,
apart from vodka and tea with flies in it, there isn't a thing
to be had. Drinking with not a morsel to eat is worse than
nothing."

"Yes, it wouldn't be a bad idea to have a little something
now," agreed Ivan Ivanitch Dvoetochiev, inspector of ecclesi-
astical schools, muffling himself from the wind in his rust-
coloured overcoat. "It's two o'clock already and the taverns
are shut but some herrings wouldn't be a bad idea . . . or mush-
rooms, say . . . or something of the sort, you know . . ."

He waggled his fingers in the air and sketched a sort of dish
across his face, a very savoury one, no doubt, for everybody
looking licked their lips. The group came to a halt and began
thinking. They thought and thought but couldn't think up
anything to eat: they had to confine themselves only to
dreams.

"At Golopesov's one splendid evening I ate turkey!" sighed
Prujina-Prujinski, Assistant Police Commissioner. "By the
way . . . you were in Warsaw some time or other, weren't you,
gentlemen? They do this there . . . They take ordinary carp,
alive . . . and frisky and put 'em in milk . . . For a day the
things swim about in milk and then they fry them in sour
cream in the pan just so . . . that then, my friend, you can keep
your pineapples! My God! Especially if you drink a glass and
then another. You eat . . . in a sort of oblivion. You can't feel
it . . . Just from the aroma you could die!"

"And if you've salted cucumbers too . . ." added Rebrotycsov
with heartfelt fellow-feeling. "When we were stationed in Po-
land . . . we used to have those meat dumplings two hundred
at a time in a stew . . . You'd a full plateful of them, shook on
pepper, strewed fennel and parsley . . . There's no word to
describe it!"

Suddenly Rebrotyesov stopped and was pensive. There came
to his mind a dish of sturgeon that he ate in 1856 at the
Triatska Monastery. So savoury was his memory of that sturgeon that the garrison commander sniffed suddenly the smell
of fish and chewed unconsciously, not noticing that mud was
gathering in his galoshes.

"No, no!" He said. "I can't stand it any longer! I'm going
home to satisfy my appetite. I'll tell you what, gentlemen, you
come to my place, too. Yes, by God! We'll drink our glass and
eat whatever God provides. Cucumber, sausage . . . We'll set
up the samovar . . . What about it? we'll eat, we'll chat about
the plague, we'll remember old times . . . My wife's asleep but
we won't go and wake her . . . Quietly then . . . Come on!"

There is no need to describe the enthusiasm with which the
invitation was received. I will only say that never was such
good will shown to Rebrotyesov as on that night.

❖ ❖ ❖

"I'll box your ears!" said the garrison commander to his batman as he led his guest into the dark hall. "I've told you a
thousand times, you scoundrel, to burn sweet-smelling tissues

when you sleep in the hall. Go and set up the samovar, you idiot, and tell Irina she'd better bring . . . some cucumber and radish from the larder . . . Yes, and prepare some herrings . . . Crumble some spring onions with them, yes, and strew fennel . . . you know . . . and slice potatoes in a circle round . . . And beetroot too . . . All together, you know, with vinegar and butter and mustard . . . Sprinkle pepper over it . . . Garnish, in fact . . . Understand?''

Rebrotyesov waddled his fingers to describe the concoction, garnishing in mime what he could not garnish in words. His guests took off their galoshes and went into a dark room. The master of the house struck a match, diffusing sulphur, and lit up walls decked with prizes from *Neva*,* views of Venice and portraits of the writer Lajechnikov and a certain general with astonished eyes.

"In no time at all . . ." whispered Rebrotyesov, quietly taking up the table cover, ". . . I'll lay the table and we'll be seated . . . My Masha was rather sick today . . . Please excuse her . . . One of these women's things . . . Dr. Goosin says it's from the lenten fare she eats . . . May well be! 'Darling,' I tell her, 'it's not a question of food. Not what goes in your mouth,' I say, 'but what comes out.' 'You eat lenten fare,' I tell her, 'and get upset as usual.' 'Instead of mortifying your flesh,' I say, 'better cheer up and stop complaining.' She won't listen! 'From childhood,' she says, 'this has been our discipline.' "

The batman came in and, craning his neck, whispered something in his master's ear. Rebrotyesov raised his eyebrows.

"Ah yes . . ." he murmured. "H'm . . . That so . . . But it's nothing, though . . . I'll put that right in a minute. Masha, don't you see, has locked the larder and the cupboards to keep the servants out and she has the keys. I'll have to go and get them . . ."

Rebrotyesov rose on tiptoe, quietly opened the door and went to his wife. She was asleep.

---

* A newspaper.

"Manechka," he said, stealthily approaching the bed, "Manechka, wake up a second."

"Who's there? You, is it? What do you want?"

"Manechka, here's what I'm about . . . Give me the keys, angel, and don't disturb yourself . . . Go on sleeping . . . I'll take care of them . . . I'll give them some cucumber and use up nothing more . . . In God's name! There's Dvoetochiev, you know, Prujina-Prujinski and a few more . . . All splendid people . . . Important socially . . . Prujinski has the order of Vladimir, even, fourth class . . . He's a high regard for you . . ."

"Where've you been slobbering?"

"Now then, you're getting angry already . . . You're like that, it's true . . . I'll give them cucumber, that'll be all . . . And they'll go . . . I'll take charge of everything and not disturb you . . . Stay in bed, my little doll . . . And how are you feeling now? Was Dr. Goosin here without me? There, I kiss your hand, see . . . And the guests have such a high regard for you . . . Dvoetochiev is a devout man, you know . . . Prujina is paymaster too . . . They all think a lot of you . . . 'Maria,' they say, 'Maria Patrovna, she's not just a lady,' they say, 'but something quite wonderful . . . the high light of our society.' "

"Come to bed and stop your fussing! Slobbering with your cronies at the club and then blabbering all night! You ought to be ashamed! You have children!"

"Yes . . . I have children, but don't upset yourself, Manechka . . . don't grieve . . . I embrace and love you . . . And the children, God knows, I'm attached to them. I take Mitya to the high school, don't I? . . . I couldn't have done more to send them packing . . . It's awkward . . . They followed me and asked for food. 'Give us something to eat,' they said. Dvoetochiev, Prujina-Prujinski . . . such nice people . . . They're fond of you, they appreciate you. Give them some cucumber and a drink . . . and be content . . . I'll take charge . . ."

"Oh, the torment of it! Have you gone crazy or what? Guests like that at this time? They ought to be ashamed, the devil take them, disturbing people at night! Where in the world do

you see guests turning up at night? Aren't there taverns here
for them? I'd be an idiot giving you the keys. Let them go and
have a sleep and come back tomorrow."

"H'm . . . You would say that . . . But I won't abase myself
before you . . . It's clear and plain you're not the comfort of
your husband, the lifelong friend of which the Scriptures speak
. . . It's disgustingly evident . . . You were a little viper and you
are still!"

"Ah! So you can abuse me still, can you, pest that you are?"

"*Merci* . . . I read the truth once in one of the papers: 'Among
other people she's an angel, not a woman, but at home with
her husband, a she-devil.' It's the solemn truth . . . You were
a devil and you're a devil still . . ."

"Take that, you!"

"Go on, go on! Beat your own husband! Well, I'll get down
on my knees and beg to you . . . I implore you, Manechka!
Forgive me! . . . Give me the keys! Manechka! Angel! Don't
put me to shame before society! My wild barbarian woman,
how long will you torment me? Go on . . . Beat me . . . *Merci*
. . . I'll entreat you just the same!"

❖ ❖ ❖

The married couple conversed a long time in this fashion.
Rebrotyesov got down on his knees, twice burst into tears,
railed at himself and kept scratching his cheek . . . It ended
when his wife got up, spat and said:

"I see there's going to be no end to my torment! Give me
my dress from the chair, Mahomet!"

Rebrotyesov carefully passed her the dress and, setting his
hair in place, went to his guests. They were standing in front
of the general's portrait, staring at his astonished eyes, and
debating the question which was of higher rank, the general
or the writer. Dvoetochiev took the part of Lajechnikov, the
writer, urging his immortality. Prujinski, however, said:

"The man's a writer. Let's say a good one, we won't argue.
And he writes with humour and sympathy. But send him off

to war and he can't cope there with the troops. Yet give a general a full army corps, why, it's nothing to him . . ."

"My Masha will be here right away . . ." said Rebrotyesov, coming in and interrupting the discussion. "Just a minute . . ."

"We're putting you to trouble, aren't we? . . . Fedor Akim-itch, what's the matter with your cheek? My dear chap, you've a black eye! Where did you land yourself with that?"

"My cheek? Where on my cheek?" muttered Rebrotyesov in confusion. "Ah yes! I sneaked in to Manechka just now, I wanted to give her a fright and all of a sudden in the darkness I bumped into the bed. Ha ha! . . . But here is Manechka . . . What a tousle-head you look, Manechka mine! A real Louise Michel!"

Maria Petrovna came into the dining room, tousled and sleepy but radiant and cheerful.

"How kind of you to call!" she said. "If you couldn't come by day, then thank my husband for bringing you at any rate by night. I was asleep just now and heard a voice . . . Who could it be? I thought . . . Fedor wanted me to stay in bed and not come out to you, but, well, I couldn't resist . . ."

She hurried out to the kitchen and the supper began . . .

❖ ❖ ❖

"How wonderful to be married!" sighed Prujina-Prujinski, leaving the garrison commander's house an hour later with the others. "You eat when you like and drink when you feel like it . . . You know there's a fellow creature who loves you . . . And plays something for you on the piano . . . Rebrotye-sov's a happy man!"

Dvoetochiev was silent. He sighed and brooded. When he arrived home and was undressing, he sighed so loudly that he woke his wife.

"Don't make such a row with you boots, you oaf!" said his wife. "You won't let a person sleep. Gallivanting at the club and then making this racket! You're a fine specimen!"

"All you know is how to quarrel!" moaned the inspector of schools. "You ought to see how Rebrotyesov and his wife live!

By God, they do live! Watch them and you feel like weeping, it's so endearing. My only misery is that you've been born on this earth to torment me. Move over!"

The inspector of schools covered himself with the quilt and, brooding on his fate, fell asleep.

1884

The Mask

❖ ❖ ❖

In the social club at X they were holding a masked ball for charity, or, as local ladies said, "a ball for pairing off."

It was midnight. Some intellectuals, not dancing and without masks—five in number—sat at a big table in the reading room, noses and beards buried in newspapers, reading, dozing, and in the word of a liberal journalist, the local correspondent of a national newspaper, "ruminating."

From the ballroom came the sounds of a quadrille; and waiters with patter of feet and rattle of plates, kept running past the door. But in the room itself there was silence.

"Be cosier in here, I think!" said a low, raucous voice, seeming suddenly to come out of the stove. "In here, then! In here, my dears!"

The door opened and into the reading room walked a broad, squat, masked man in a coachman's jacket and a cap with a peacock's feather; there followed two masked ladies and a footman carrying a tray with a thick flagon, three bottles of red wine and some glasses.

"Come on, it'll be cooler here," said the man. "Put the tray on the table. Be seated, Mademoiselles, *je vous en prie*! And you gentlemen move off . . . Nothing for you here!"

The man staggered forward and thrust some newspapers from the table.

"Put it here! And you gentlemen, reading there, make yourselves scarce! Newspapers, politics, waste of time! Chuck 'em away!"

"Will you be quiet, please," said one of the intellectuals, looking through his spectacles at the mask. "This is a reading room, not a bar . . . It's not a place for drinking."

"And why not? Is the table going to rock or the ceiling fall? Funny business . . . But I've no time for chatter. Chuck those papers away! . . . You've had your little read and that'll do. You're brainy enough without it and it damages your eyes . . . And the plain fact is: I don't want all this lot here!"

The footman put the tray on the table, laid his serviette across his elbow and stood by the door. And at the same time the ladies took their places for wine.

"What a clever lot: they prefer newspapers to a stiff drink!" said the man with the peacock's feather, filling his glass. "But it's my opinion, my dear sirs, that you're so fond of reading because you haven't the wherewithal to drink. Am I right? Ha ha! . . . Reading. Well, what is it that's written there? You sir, in glasses! What facts are you after with your reading? Ha ha! Well, throw it away! It'll turn your head! Drinking's better!"

The man with a peacock's feather stretched out and tore the newspaper from the hands of the gentleman in glasses. The latter went white, then red, and stared with astonishment at the other intellectuals—and they at him.

"You forget yourself, my dear sir!" he snapped. "You're turning this reading room into a public house, behaving in this rascally fashion, tearing newspapers from people's hands! I won't put up with it! You don't know whom you're dealing with, my dear sir! I'm Jestyakov, the banker!"

"Don't give a damn if you are . . . Jestyakov! Your newspaper indeed! Well, there's an honour . . . !"

The man took the newspaper and tore it into shreds.

"Gentlemen, what's going on?" spluttered Jestyakov. "It's very odd . . . It's quite extraordinary . . ."

"They're getting angry . . ." laughed the man. "Tra la la! And getting scared! Just shaking in their shoes! That's the way of things, my fine gentlemen! But joking apart, I don't want to talk to you. I want to be alone with these young ladies. I want to give myself a little satisfaction. So I ask you not to stand on ceremony and be off . . . Please! Mr. Bielebookhov, off you go . . . in the name of pigs! What you wriggling your snout for? I said, be off, didn't I, so be off! Quick, look lively, or perhaps you'll get it in the neck!"

"What is all this?" asked Bielebookhov, treasurer for wards of court, going red and shrugging his shoulders. "I just don't understand . . . This rascal comes bursting in here and then there's all this fuss!"

"What do you mean, rascal?" shouted the man with a peacock's feather, beating his fist in such rage on the table that the glasses shook on the tray. "Who are you talking to? Do you think because I wear a mask that you can bandy words with me? What cheek! You'll go when I tell you! Bank manager, make yourself well and truly scarce! Everybody out till not a villain of you's left! In the name of pigs!"

"Well, we'll see about that straightaway!" said Jestyakov, his glasses misty with agitation. "I'll show you! Eh there, call the officer on duty!"

A minute later there came in, out of breath from dancing, a little red-haired man with a blue ribbon in his lapel.

"I must ask you to leave!" he began. "This room is not for drinking! Please go to the bar!"

"Why do you say that, old chap?" asked the man in a mask. "Did I call you at all?"

"I must ask you not to be familiar and to go!"

"Well, my dear man, I'll give you just one minute . . . Because you're in charge here, see these fellows through the door. My young ladies don't like having any strangers here . . . They're shy and I want them in a natural fettle for my money's worth."

"Obviously the stupid man doesn't realise he's not in a pigsty!" shouted Jestyakov. "Call Yevstrat Spiridonitch!"

"Yevstrat Spiridonitch!" rang through the club. "Where's Yevstrat Spiridonitch?"

Yevstrat Spiridonitch, an old man in Police officer's uniform, was not slow to appear.

"I must ask you to leave here!" he wheezed, glaring fierce-eyed and waggling his dyed moustaches.

"Look, he's scared!" said the man in a mask and chuckled with satisfaction. "He he! Scared! Did you ever see such a funk, God strike me down! Whiskers like a cat and eyes a-goggle! He he he!"

"I must ask you not to be obstinate!" shouted Yevstrat Spiridonitch with all his strength and started trembling. "Be off! I order you to remove yourself!"

An incredible hubbub arose in the reading room. Yevstrat Spiridonitch, red as a lobster, shouted and stamped. Jestyakov shouted. Bielebookhov shouted. All the intellectuals shouted, but louder than all the voices sounded the low, thick, raucous bass of the man in the mask. Dancing stopped in general uproar and people flocked into the reading room.

Yevstrat Spiridonitch called for all the Police officers in the club and sat down to write a report.

"Write away, write away!" said the masked man, poking his finger under the pen. "Now what's in store for poor me? I'm done for. Why are you going to ruin me, a poor orphan? Ha ha! Why indeed? Report ready? All written out? Well then, look! One . . . Two . . . Three!"

The man got up, stretched to his full height and plucked off his mask. His drunken face revealed and looking at them all, he fell into an armchair and laughed with delight. And indeed the effect was extraordinary. All the intellectuals looked at one another in confusion and went pale, some clawing their heads. Yevstrat Spiridonitch yelped like someone committing inadvertently a terrible blunder.

Everybody recognized the rogue: a local millionaire and factory owner, Pyatigorov, a citizen of high degree by birth, famed for scandal, philanthropy, and, as was often said, a love of culture.

"Well, are you going or aren't you?" asked Pyatigorov after a minute's silence.

Quietly, without a word, the intellectuals tip-toed from the reading room and Pyatigorov locked the door behind them.

"You knew, didn't you, that it was Pyatigorov!" muttered Yevstrat Spiridonitch under his breath, shaking by the shoulders the footman who brought in the wine. "Why did you keep quiet?"

"I wasn't ordered to say anything!"

"You weren't ordered . . . Well then, I'll lock you up for a month and you'll understand what you weren't ordered! Be off! And as for you, gentlemen . . ."—he turned to the intellectuals—". . . you've made a fine mess . . . They won't be out of the room for ten minutes or thereabouts. So sort it out for yourselves. Oh, gentlemen, gentlemen . . . I don't like it, by God I don't!"

The intellectuals went dejectedly about the club, embarrassed, guilty, whispering together with sharp sense of impending trouble. Their wives and daughters, aware that Pyatigorov was offended and angered by it, became quiet and began to leave for home. There was no more dancing . . .

At two o'clock Pyatigorov came out of the reading room. He was staggering drunkenly. He made his way into the ballroom, sat down near the orchestra and dozed off to the music; then mournfully bowed his head and snored.

"Don't play!" Stewards gestured to the musicians. "Hush! . . . Yegor Illitch is asleep . . ."

"Wouldn't you like to be taken home, Yegor Illitch?" asked Bielebookhov, bending to the millionaire's ear.

Pyatigorov twitched his lips as if to blow a fly from his cheek.

"Wouldn't you like to be taken home," repeated Bielebookhov, "or have the coachman called to the door?"

"Eh . . . ? Who . . . ? What . . . you want . . . ?"

"Like to go home . . . ? Time for bye-byes . . ."

"I want to go home . . . Take me!"

Bielebookhov beamed with satisfaction and started to lift

Pyatigorov. The other intellectuals came rushing up and with pleasant smiles bore out the citizen of high degree and carried him to his carriage.

"Only a man of talent, an artist, could have fooled all the company like this," said Jestyakov cheerfully, setting him down. "I was literally floored, Yegor Illitch! I've gone on laughing till this very moment! . . . Ha ha! . . . Didn't we work ourselves up and make a fuss! Ha ha! Would you believe it? In a theatre I've never laughed as much . . . The height of comedy! All my life I shall remember this immortal evening!"

With Pyatigorov away, the intellectuals cheered up and were calmer.

"He gave me his hand as we said goodbye," declared Jestyakov, highly delighted. "So it doesn't matter. He's not angry."

"Thank God!" sighed Yevstrat Spiridonitch. "He's a ruffian, a most unpleasant fellow, but all the same . . . a public benefactor! Quite impossible!"

1884

A TERRIBLE NIGHT

❖ ❖ ❖

Ivan Petrovitch Panikhidin went pale, turned down the lamp and spoke with deep feeling:

"A dark shadow lay over the land that Christmas Eve in 1883 as I made my way home from the house of a friend, now dead, where we had taken part in a seance. The lane I had to go along was unlit and I made my way almost by touch. My room in Moscow was in a large boarding house owned by Troopov, a civil servant, in a very dreary district. My thoughts, as I moved forward, were gloomy and oppressive . . .

" 'Your life is ebbing to its close . . . Go to confession.' "

"Those were the words spoken to me by Spinoza, the spirit we had dared to conjure up. I asked him to repeat them and the saucer not only did so but added: 'Tonight.' I don't believe in spiritualism but the thought of death, even in casual reference, depresses me. Death, gentlemen, is unavoidable, common to all, but nevertheless repugnant to the nature of man . . . And now, as cold darkness gathered about me, raindrops whirling furiously in moaning wind, with not a living soul to see, no human sound to hear, a vague and inexplicable terror came upon me. I, a man quite free from superstition, hurried forward, afraid to look back or glance to the side. I felt that, if I did, I would surely see death in ghostly form."

Panikhidin breathed deeply, drank some water and went on:

"This vague but very natural terror didn't leave me even as I climbed to the fourth floor of Troopov's boarding house, opened my door and went into the room. It was dark in my modest dwelling and a soft wind moaned above the stove and, as if seeking warmth, rattled the air-vent.

" 'If we're to believe Spinoza . . .' "—I smiled ironically— '. . . then, there, beneath that stove, my death will come tonight . . . A rather horrible thought, though!'

"I lit a match . . . Frantic gusts of wind scurried over the roof of the building. The quiet moaning became a low spiteful howl and somewhere down below a loose shutter clattered . . .

" 'How grim it must be for homeless people on a night like this . . .' I thought.

"But there was no time to ponder in this way. As the sulphur of my match flared in little blue flame, I glanced round the room and an astonishing and terrible sight confronted me . . . If only a gust of wind had blown out the match! Then perhaps I'd have seen nothing and the hairs would not have reared up on my head. I gave a cry, stepped back towards the door and, full of horror, shut my eyes . . .

"In the middle of the room was a coffin.

"In the brief blue flame I had made out its shape . . . had seen silk brocade, pink and shimmering with glints . . . and a cross of fretted gold on top. Some things, gentlemen, impress themselves on the memory, even if we see them only for a moment. So it was with that coffin. I saw it only for a second or two but I remember its slightest features . . . It was for someone of medium height and, to judge by the pink colour, a young girl. The expensive brocade, the supports, the bronze handles—all suggested that she was rich.

"I ran headlong from my room and without reflection, without thought, knowing only fear, rushed down the stairs. In the dark my legs got tangled in the skirts of my overcoat: it's a wonder I didn't fall and break my neck. I came out into the street, leaned against a wet lamppost and tried to compose myself. My heart was beating fearfully and I couldn't get my breath . . ."

One of the listeners turned up the lamp and moved closer to the storyteller who continued:

"To find my room on fire, or a thief there, or a mad dog . . . that wouldn't have astounded me. Nor would it if the ceiling had come down, the floor caved in or the walls given way. Those are natural phenomena and can be understood. But how could a coffin have come in my room? Where could it have come from? . . . Expensive, for a young woman of high rank apparently—how could it have come to the dingy room of a petty clerk? Was it empty, or was there . . . a dead body in it? *Who was she*, then, taken prematurely from a life of riches to pay me this strange and terrible visit? It was an agonizing mystery!

" 'If this is not a supernatural thing . . .'—the thought flashed into my mind—'then it must be a crime . . .'

"I was lost in wonder and conjecture. My door had been locked when I was out and only my closest friends knew where the key was. Friends wouldn't bring me a coffin. Perhaps undertaker's men brought it there by mistake, chose the wrong floor or wrong door and put the coffin where it wasn't intended. But it's well known that undertaker's men don't leave a room before they're paid or at least given a tip.

" 'The spirits foretold my death.' I remembered. 'Did they provide a coffin too?'

"Gentlemen, I do not believe in spirits, nor did I then, but a coincidence of that sort would put even a philosopher into a sombre mood.

" 'But this is all nonsense!' I decided. 'I'm as frightened as a schoolboy. It was an optical illusion—nothing more! I was feeling so gloomy when I came in, no wonder my strained nerves made me imagine a coffin . . . Of course, an optical illusion. What else could it have been?'

"The rain lashed my face and battered my cap and the skirts of my overcoat . . . I was cold and fearfully wet . . . I had to go somewhere . . . But where? To go back to my room might mean seeing the coffin again and that sight would be more than I could stand. To be alone with a coffin, perhaps with a dead body inside it, when there wasn't a living soul to see, no human sound to hear . . . : it could cost me my reason . . . But to stay in the street in the cold and pouring rain was out of the question.

"I decided to go and spend the night with my friend Upokoev, who later shot himself, you'll remember. He lived in furnished rooms in the house of Cherepov, the merchant, on Dead Street."

Panikhidin wiped perspiration from his pale face and, with a sigh, continued:

"I didn't find my friend at home. When I had knocked till I was sure he wasn't there, I groped for the key over the door, opened it and went in. I flung my wet overcoat to the floor and, stumbling against a dim sofa, sat down on it to rest . . . It was very dark . . . The wind droned mournfully in the ventilator shaft and in the stove a cricket chirped a monotonous song. From the Kremlin came the peal of Christmas bells . . . I hurriedly lit a match. But its light did not lighten my gloom—quite the reverse. A fearful horror once again overwhelmed me. I cried out, reeled and, not knowing what I did, ran from the room . . .

"For in my friend's flat, as in my own, there was—a coffin!

"It was almost twice as big as mine and its brown upholstery gave it a particularly sombre hue. How had it come there? My eyes were deceiving me—impossible to doubt that any longer. There couldn't be a coffin in both rooms. It must be a sickness of the nerves, an hallucination. Wherever I went now, I would see before my death's terrible dwelling place. Perhaps I'd gone out of my mind, was suffering from a kind of 'coffin-mania,' and the cause of that madness wasn't hard to find: I had only to remember the spiritualist seance and Spinoza's words . . .

" 'I'm going mad!' I thought in horror, clutching my brow. 'My God! What will become of me?'

"I'd a splitting headache and my legs were giving way . . .

The rain was pouring down in bucketfuls, there was a piercing wind and now I had neither fur coat nor cap. To go back to the flat for them was out of the question, quite beyond my powers ... Terror clutched me fiercely in an icy grip. Even though I knew I had suffered an hallucination, the hairs rose up on my head and sweat poured from my brow ...''

"What was I to do?" went on Panikhidin. "I was out of my wits and likely to catch my death of cold. Luckily I remembered that a good friend lived not far from Dead Street: Pogostov, a doctor recently qualified, who had been with me that evening at the seance. I hurried to his dwelling ... At that time he wasn't yet married to his rich wife and lived on the fifth floor of the big boarding house owned by Kladbishenski, the counsellor of state.

"There my overwrought nerves were to suffer further torment. As I climbed to the fifth floor, I heard a terrible noise. Someone was running overhead, thudding heavily and slamming doors.

" 'Help me!' I heard a heart-rending cry. 'Help me! Caretaker!'

"And a moment later there came down the stairs towards me a dark figure in fur coat and flabby top hat.

" 'Pogostov!' I shouted, as I recognized my friend. 'It's you. What's the matter?'

"As he reached me, Pogostov stopped and clutched my arm convulsively. He was pale, breathing heavily and trembling. His eyes were distracted and his chest heaved ...

" 'Is it you, Panikhidin?' he asked in hollow voice. 'But is it really you? You're as pale as if you'd come from the grave ... But enough of that ... You're not an hallucination, are you? ... My God! You look terrible!'

" 'And what about you? You look pretty awful.'

" 'Oh, my dear chap, give me time to pull myself together ... I'm glad to see you, if it's really you and not an optical illusion. That damned seance! ... It shook up my nerves so much that, imagine, as soon as I got home, I saw ... there in my room ... a coffin!'

"I couldn't believe my ears and asked him to repeat what he'd said.

" 'A coffin, a real coffin!' said the doctor, sitting down, quite worn out, on a step. 'I'm not a coward but the devil himself would be scared if, after a seance, he stumbled on a coffin in the dark.'

"Confused and trying to console him a little, I told the doctor about the coffins that I had seen . . .

"For a minute we stared at one another, wide-eyed and open-mouthed. Then, to convince ourselves we weren't hallucinations, we started to punch each other.

" 'It's hurting both of us,' said the doctor. 'That means we're not asleep and seeing one another in dreams. So the coffins, mine and both of yours, can't be illusions but really do exist. Well, what do we do now, old chap?'

"We stayed a full hour on the cold staircase, then decided, lost in wonder and conjecture and terribly cold, to cast off our mean fears, wake up the caretaker and go with him to the doctor's room. We did so. As we went in, we lit a candle and at once saw a coffin upholstered in white silk brocade with gold fringes and tassels. The caretaker piously crossed himself.

" 'Now we can find out . . .' said the pallid doctor, his body trembling, '. . . whether this coffin is empty . . . or occupied . . .'

"After long hesitation, very natural in the circumstances, the doctor stooped and, gritting his teeth in fearful expectation, pulled off the coffin lid. We looked in and . . .

"It was *empty* . . .

"Instead of a dead body we found a letter which read as follows:

" 'Dear Pogostov,

" 'You know that my father-in-law has got his business into a fearful mess. He's up to the ears in debt. Tomorrow or the day after there will be distraint on his goods, and that will ruin his family and mine, and stain our honour too, which I hold more dear. At a family conference last night we decided to put away all things of value. Since my father-in-law's property consists of coffins—as you know, he's a master coffin-maker, the best in town—we decided to conceal all the best coffins. I implore you as a friend to help us save our property and honour. In the hope that you can store our property I am bringing you, my dear fellow, one coffin which I beg you to conceal in your room till I can take it back. I hope you will not refuse me, especially as the coffin will not be with you for more than a week. To all whom I count our sincere friends I am sending a coffin and putting my trust in their generosity and kindness.

" 'Your dear friend,
" 'Ivan Cheloustin.'

"For three months after this terrible experience I was treated for nervous exhaustion; and our friend, the coffin-maker's son-in-law, saved both his property and honour. He has a monumental mason's business now and trades in tombstones and memorial tablets. He is not doing very well and every night, when I come home, I fear that I'll see beside my bed a statue in white marble or a catafalque."

1884

THE CROW

❖ ❖ ❖

It was not later than six in the evening when Lieutenant Strekachev, strolling through town, happened to look up at some pink curtains on the first floor of a big, three-storied building.

"That's where Madame Doudou lives . . ." he remembered. "A long time since I was at her place. Shall I drop in?"

But before making up his mind Strekachev pulled a purse from his pocket and peered nervously into it. He saw a crumbled rouble note, smelling of kerosene, a button, two copecks—and that was all.

"Not much . . . Well, never mind!" he decided. "I'll call just the same, sit around for a bit."

A minute later and Strekachev was already in the anteroom and breathing deep into his chest the smell of perfume and of soap of glycerine. Another smell too, impossible to define, but which you always find in girls' so-called bachelor apartments, a mixture of female scents and male cigars. From the hall stand hung some overcoats and raincoats and a glossy top hat.

Going further in, the lieutenant saw again what he had seen the previous year: a piano with broken keys, a vase of withered flowers, a stain of spilt drink on the floor. A door led into the

drawing room, another to the room where Doudou slept or
played at piquet with Brondi, an old teacher of dancing, who
looked very like Offenbach. If you glanced into the drawing
room, you saw a door at the opposite side and through it the
side of a bed with pink muslin curtains. Here lived Mesdames
Doudou, Barbe and Blanche who called themselves "dancing
mistresses."

There was no one in the anteroom. The lieutenant moved
into the drawing room and there confronted someone. Behind
a round table, sprawling on a sofa, was a young man with bris-
tly hair and dim, blue eyes, a cold sweat on his brow, and the
expression of one who has crawled out of a dark and terrible,
deep pit. He was foppishly dressed in a new, knitted suit that
still bore traces of pressing; a pendant dangled on his chest;
and on his feet were patent leather, buckled boots and red
stockings. He was propping up his plump cheeks with his fists
and looking wanly at a little bottle of seltzer water in front of
him. On another table were a few bottles and a plate of oranges.

When he saw the lieutenant, the dandy stared and gaped.
Strekachev stepped a pace back in surprise . . . With difficulty
he recognized in the dandy his military clerk Filenkov, whom
only that morning he had scolded in the office for illiterate
spelling, for writing "cobage" instead of "cabbage."

Filenkov slowly raised himself and set his hands on the
table. For a minute he did not take his eyes from the lieutenant's face and even turned a little blue with inner strain.

"What are you doing here?" Strekachev asked him sternly.

"Your honour . . . I . . ." muttered the clerk, lowering his
eyes. ". . . It's a birthday . . . When there's general conscription
. . . and they take everybody . . . just the same . . ."

"I asked what you were doing here?" The lieutenant raised
his voice. "And what sort of dress is that?"

"Your honour, I feel I've done wrong but . . . if they take
everybody . . . with general conscription . . . equally . . . I'm an
educated man, I can't visit Mademoiselle Barbe on her birthday in a low-rank uniform, so naturally I put on the sort of
dress I wear at home, that is, that of a gentleman . . ."

Noticing the lieutenant's eyes become angrier, Filenkov fell silent and lowered his head as if expecting a sudden blow. The lieutenant opened his mouth to say, "Be off with you!" but, as he did so, a blonde in bright yellow house-coat came in, eyebrows raised. Recognizing the lieutenant, she screeched and flung herself at him.

"Vasha! An officer!"

Seeing that Barbe (who was one of Madame Doudou's ladies) was on familiar terms with the lieutenant, the clerk pulled himself together and livened up. Spreading his fingers, he lifted himself from the table, then waved his arms.

"Your honour!" he began, swallowing. "It is my privilege to congratulate a dear person on her birthday. You wouldn't find her equal in Paris! Really! A dazzler! I didn't grudge the three hundred roubles, I had that house-coat made for this dear person on her birthday. Champagne, your honour. Let's drink her health on her birthday!"

"And where is Blanche?" asked the lieutenant.

"She's just coming, your honour," replied the military clerk, although the question was not to him but to Barbe. "Straight-away! A splendid girl . . . *à la* . . . *Comprenez . . . Au revoir . . . Consommé . . .*" The other day a merchant from Kostroma came here and paid five hundred roubles . . . No small thing, five hundred! I'm being familiar only out of particular respect! Am I being presumptuous? Please have a drink, your honour!"

The clerk gave a glass of champagne to the lieutenant and to Barbe and he himself drank vodka. The lieutenant drank, then collected himself.

"You're taking liberties, I see," he said. "Be off with you and tell Demianov to put you in the guard room for a day."

"Your honour . . . Yes, perhaps you think I'm some sort of swine . . . ? Do you think that? Oh, my God! And my dad a gentleman by birth, given honours! As for me, if you'd like to know, a general was my godfather. Do you think that, because I'm a clerk, I must be a swine? . . . Please . . . have another little glass of bubbly . . . Barbe, come on! Don't hold back, we can pay for it all. Modern education makes us all equal. A general's son or a merchant's is called up just like a peasant's. I went to high school, your honour, and grammar school and college . . . Everywhere they turned me out! Come on then, Barbe! Take another drink and shame the common herd! Your honour, another little drink!"

Madame Doudou came in, a big, plump, hawk-faced woman. Behind her moved Brondi, looking like Offenbach. A little later, Blanche came too, a small brunette of nineteen with severe face and Grecian nose, evidently Jewish. The military clerk proposed another round.

"Fire water for everybody! Let's light up! Let me smash this vase! For the pleasure of it!"

Madame Doudou started to say that a decent girl knows how to behave, that it's not respectable for girls to drink, and that, if she allowed her girls to drink, it was only because she relied on the men behaving themselves, and, if they didn't, she wouldn't have them there.

From the drink and the nearness of Blanche the lieutenant's head began to spin and he forgot about the military clerk.

"Music!" shouted the clerk, despair in his voice. "Let's have some music! According to Regulation 120 I call on you to dance! Si-silence!" He yelled at the top of his voice, thinking it wasn't himself who was shouting but someone else. "Si-silence! I want some dancing. You must respect my disposition. I'm going to foot it, foot it!"

Barbe and Blanche consulted Madame Doudou. Old Brondi sat at the piano. Dancing began. Filenkov stamped to the beat, watched the movements of four female legs and neighed with pleasure.

"Go it! That's the way! With feeling! Let it rip! Swing it!"

After a time they all went in carriages to the Arcadia, Filenkov with Barbe, the lieutenant with Blanche and Brondi with Madame Doudou.

They took a table there and ordered supper. Filenkov drank so much he lost his voice and couldn't move his hands. He sat gloomily blinking his eyes, as if about to cry, and said:

"Who am I? What sort of man? I'm a crow!"

He mimicked himself: "A gentleman . . . You're a crow . . . no gentleman."

The lieutenant, befuddled by drink, scarcely noticed him. Just once, seeing his drunken face in a mist, he frowned and said:

"You're taking liberties, I see . . ."

But then he couldn't think it through and clinked glasses with him.

From the Arcadia they went to Krestovski Garden. There Madame Doudou said goodbye to the younger couples, saying she counted on the men behaving themselves and went off with Brondi. Then they ordered fresh coffee with brandy and liqueurs. Then kvass and vodka and caviare. The clerk smeared his face with caviare and said:

"Now I'm an Arab or one of the Devil's brood."

Next morning the lieutenant, his head like lead and his mouth burning and dry, went to his office. Filenkov was sitting in his place in clerk's uniform and rustling some papers together with trembling hands. His face was dark, not smooth, like a cobblestone, his bristling hair stuck out in different directions and he could hardly keep his eyes open. When he saw the lieutenant, he rose heavily, took a deep breath and pulled himself to attention. The lieutenant, bitter and in no mood for more drinking, turned away and got on with his work. For ten minutes there was silence but then his eyes met the lacklustre ones of the clerk and in them he saw it all: the red curtains, the wild dance, the Arcadia, the profile of Blanche . . .

"With general conscription . . ." muttered Filenkov, ". . . when even professors are taken to be soldiers . . . when everybody's equal . . . and even civil rights . . ."

The lieutenant wanted to punish him, to hand him over to the Sergeant, but he lifted his hand and said quietly:

"To the devil with you!"

And he left the office.

1885

THE BOOTS

❖ ❖ ❖

Mirkin, the piano-tuner, clean-shaven, with yellow face, tobacco-stained nose and cotton wool in his ears, came out into the corridor, calling plaintively.

"Simeon! Boots!"

And you might have thought from his frightened face that the plaster had fallen on him or he'd just seen a ghost in his room.

"Simeon, for pity's sake!" he cried, seeing the boots come running. "What's all this then? I suffer from rheumatism, I'm a sick man, and you're forcing me to go out barefoot! Why haven't you given me my boots by this time? Where are they?"

Simeon went into Mirkin's room, looked where he usually put the finished boots and scratched his head. The boots weren't there.

"Now where are they, cursed things?" said Simeon. "Seems last night I cleaned them and put them there ... H'm ... Yesterday I was tight, I must admit. I dare say I must have put them in another room. That must be it, Afanasi Yegoritch, in another room. There's such a lot of boots and the devil mixes them up in the sight of a drunken man, if you're not careful

79

... I must have put them in the lady next door's ... the actress ..."

"Now I have to go and disturb a lady, if you please, because of you! Because of this nonsense, if you please, I have to wake up a respectable woman!"

Sighing and coughing, Mirkin went to the door of the next room and carefully knocked.

"Who's there?" came a woman's voice a moment later.

"It is *I*!" began Mirkin plaintively, like an admirer addressing a lady of fashion. "Pardon me for disturbing you, Madam, but I'm a sick man, I suffer from rheumatism. Madam, my doctors have instructed me to keep my feet warm, especially as I must go at once to tune the piano for the wife of General Shevelitzin. But I can't go to her barefoot!"

"But what is it you want? What piano?"

"Not a piano, Madam. It's a matter of boots! That idiot Simeon cleaned mine and put them in your room by mistake. Madam, be so kind as to give me my boots!"

He heard a rustling, a jump from bed and a slithering of slippers, then the door opened a little and a fat, feminine hand flung a pair of boots at Mirkin's feet. The piano-tuner expressed his thanks and went back to his room.

"Funny ..." he muttered, putting on a boot. "Seems as if it's not the right boot. Yes, there are two left boots! Both left boots! Simeon, do you hear, these are not my boots. My boots have red tabs and no patches and these are torn and haven't tabs!"

Simeon picked up the boots, turned them over once or twice in front of his eyes and frowned.

"They're Pavel Alexandrovitch's boots ..." he muttered with a sidelong look.

He had a squint in his left eye.

"What Pavel Alexandrovitch?"

"The actor ... Comes here every Tuesday ... He must have put yours on instead of his ... I must have taken both pairs to her room: yours and his. A mix-up!"

"Then go and change them!"

"Fine how-do-you do!" chuckled Simeon. "Go and change them! . . . And where am I to get him now? An hour he's been gone . . . Go chase the wind in the fields!"

"Where's he live, then?"

"But who knows? He comes here every Tuesday but as for where he lives . . . unknown. He comes, spends the night . . . then wait till next Tuesday . . ."

"See what you've done, you lout! Well, what am I to do now! It's time for me to go to General Shevelitzin's wife, you reprobate! My feet will freeze!"

"It doesn't take long to change a pair of boots. Put these on, wear them till evening, and in the evening go to the theatre . . . Ask there for Blistanov, the actor . . . If you don't want to go to the theatre, then you'll have to wait till Tuesday. He only comes here on Tuesdays . . ."

"But why are there two left boots?" asked the piano-tuner, regarding them with wary distaste.

"What God sends, we have to bear. Because we're poor . . . Where are you to find that actor? . . . 'Pavel Alexandrovitch,' I say, 'these boots of yours! Disgraceful!' 'Tremble and look pale!' he says. 'In these very boots,' he says, 'have I played counts and princes.' Queer people! In a word, artists. If I were governor or some big official, I'd get all these actors . . . and put them in prison."

Groaning and scowling Mirkin pulled the two left boots on his feet and limped his way to the house of General Shevelitzin's wife. All day he walked about the town to tune pianos and all day fancied everyone was looking at his feet, seeing his boots had patches and were down at heel. Besides his mental agony there came another, physical, to try him: he got a corn.

In the evening he was at the theatre. They were playing *Bluebeard*. Just before the last act, helped by a flautist he knew, he went back stage. Going into the men's dressing room, he found all the male actors in the company there. One was changing, another making up, a third smoking. Bluebeard was standing with King Bobesh and showing him a revolver.

"Buy it!" he said. "I bought it myself in Kursk for eight, as it happens; well, I'll let you have it for six . . . Marvellous action!"

"Careful . . . It's loaded!"

"May I see Mr. Blistanov?" asked the piano-tuner as he came in.

"I'm the man himself!"—Bluebeard turned to him—"What can I do for you?"

"Please excuse me, sir, if I disturb you," pleaded the piano-tuner, "but believe me, I'm a sick man, I suffer from rheumatism. My doctors have instructed me to keep my feet warm . . ."

"But what, in fact, can I do for you?"

"Well, you see," went on the piano-tuner directly to Bluebeard, ". . . the fact is . . . last night you found yourself in Bukteev's boarding house . . . in room sixty-four . . ."

"Now then, what's all this?" chuckled King Bobesh. "My wife lives in room sixty-four!"

"Your wife? How very nice! . . ." Mirkin smiled. "She then, your wife, in fact, handed me these boots. When he"—he pointed to Bluebeard—"went away from her, I missed my boots . . . I shouted, you see, for the boots but he said: 'But, sir, I put your boots in the next room!' By mistake, when he was drunk, he put in room sixty-four my boots and yours as well . . ."—Mirkin turned to Blistanov—"but you, leaving your lady, put mine on . . ."

"What are you up to?" said Blistanov, frowning. "Coming here spreading scandal, is that it?"

"Oh, not at all! God forbid! You've misunderstood . . . What am I here about? About boots! You did happen to be in room sixty-four, didn't you?"

"When?"

"Last night."

"Did you see me there?"

"No, I didn't see you." Mirkin sat down in confusion and hurriedly pulled off his boots. "I didn't see you but your lady flung your boots out to me . . . Instead of my own, that is . . ."

"My dear sir, what right have you to make these scandalous

assertions? I don't speak for myself but you're insulting a lady, and in the presence of her husband too!"

A terrible noise sounded in the theatre. King Bobesh, the outraged husband, suddenly went purple and struck the table with such force of fist that in the dressing room next door two actresses felt ill.

"Do you believe it?" Bluebeard shouted at him. "Do you believe this scoundrel? O . . . oh! If you want, I'll kill him like a dog? Want me to? I'll make mincemeat of him! I'll bash his head in!"

And all who walked that evening in the public garden by the summer theatre now relate they saw before the final act a barefoot man come fearful from the theatre down the central path with yellow face and eyes full of horror. In pursuit of him there ran a man in Bluebeard's costume with a revolver in his hand. No one saw what happened after that. It is only known that Mirkin, after meeting Blistanov, lay ill two weeks and to the words "I am a sick man. I suffer from rheumatism," began to add "I am disabled."

1885

THE FATHER OF A FAMILY

❖ ❖ ❖

IT USUALLY HAPPENS AFTER A BIG LOSS AT CARDS OR A DRINKING bout when his catarrh is troubling him. Stepan Stepanitch Zhilin wakes in an unusually sullen temper. His look is sour, slack, crumpled; on his face is an expression of resentment: he seems offended or disgusted by something. He dresses slowly, slowly drinks his Vichy water, and starts walking about the rooms.

"I'd like to know the b-brute who's been going about and not closing doors!" he mutters angrily, wrapping himself in his dressing gown and belching loudly. "Take this paper away! What's it lying about here for? We keep twenty servants and there's less mess in a pot-house. Who's that ringing there? Who the devil is it?"

"It's Anfissa, the midwife who delivered our Fedya," replies his wife.

"Always hanging about . . . Lot of spongers!"

"There's no understanding you, Stepan Stepanitch. You asked her yourself and now you're cursing her."

"I'm not cursing, I'm speaking. Better busy yourself with something, woman, instead of sitting here, with your hands in your lap, getting into arguments! I don't understand women,

I honestly don't! I do not under-stand! The way they spend the whole day doing nothing! A man works and labours like an ox, a beast, and his wife, his life's companion, sits like a little doll, doing nothing, just waiting out of boredom for a chance to quarrel with her husband. It's time to drop these schoolgirl ways, woman. You're not a schoolgirl, not a young lady but a wife and mother! What are you turning away for? Ha ha! It isn't pleasant to hear the bitter truth!"

"Strange you only tell me the bitter truth when your liver's paining you."

"Go on, make a scene, go on . . ."

"Were you out of town yesterday? Or playing cards with someone?"

"And what if I was? Whose business is that? Am I answerable to someone? Isn't it my own money I'm losing? What I spend and what's spent in this house belongs to me! Do you hear? To me!"

And so on, all in the same tone. But at no time is Stepan Stepanitch more reasonable, virtuous, strict and righteous than at table when all his household sit about him. It usually happens with the soup. Swallowing his first spoonful, Zhilin suddenly frowns and stops drinking.

"Devil knows what this is . . ." he mutters. "I shall have to start eating in a restaurant."

"What is it?" asks his wife anxiously. "Isn't it good soup?"

"I don't know what sort of a pig's taste you need to drink this hog-wash! It's too salty, it stinks like dirty rags . . . Bugs in it instead of onions . . . Simply disgraceful, Anfissa Ivanovna . . ."—he turns to the midwife—"every day you give out a lot of money for provisions, you deny yourself, and this is what they feed you with! Obviously they want me to give up my job and go into the kitchen and cook."

"The soup's all right today . . ." remarks the governess timidly.

"Is it? So you think so?" says Zhilin, glaring at her angrily. "Well, everyone to his taste. But let's face it, Varvara Vassilyevna, you and I are altogether different in taste. For instance

the behaviour of this boy here pleases you." (With a tragic
gesture he points to his son Fedya.) "You're delighted with
him but I . . . I'm disgusted. Indeed I am!"

Fedya, a seven-year-old with pale, sick face, stops eating and
lowers his eyes. He goes paler still.

"Oh yes! You're delighted with him but I'm disgusted . . . I
don't know who is right but I venture to think that as a father
I know my own son better than you do. Look how he's sitting
now. Do well-brought-up children sit like that? Sit properly."

Fedya lifts up his chin and cranes his neck and sits in what
he thinks is a better way. Tears well up in his eyes.

"Eat! Hold your spoon properly! Wait, I'll give you what for,
you nasty child! Don't you dare cry! Look straight at me!"

Fedya tries to look straight at him but his face quivers and
tears run from his eyes.

"Ha ha! You're crying are you? You're in the wrong and still
you cry. Go and stand in the corner, you brute!"

"But . . . let him eat his dinner first!" his wife intervenes.

"He'll have no dinner! Such a ruffi . . . Naughty boys like
him have no right to a dinner."

Wincing, all his body quivering, Fedya creeps down from
the chair and goes to the corner.

"You won't get away with that!" continues his father. "If
nobody cares to bring you up properly, very well, I shall begin
. . . With me, my lad, there'll be no naughtiness and crying at
table! Blockhead! You have duties! Do you understand? Duties! Your father works and so must you! No one has a right
to bread for doing nothing. You have to be a man. A M-A-N!"

"Stop, for God's sake!" begs his wife in French. "Don't
shame us before other people. The old woman can hear everything, and now, thanks to her, all the town will know . . ."

"I'm not afraid of other people," replies Zhilin in Russian.
"Anfissa Ivanovna can see I'm speaking the truth. Well, do
you think, then, I should be satisfied with this boy? Do you
know how much he costs me? Do you know, nasty little fellow
that you are, how much you cost me? Or do you think I
manufacture money or that they give it me for doing nothing?

Don't start howling! Silence! Do you hear or do you not? Or
do you want me to thrash you, you villain!"

Fedya gives a loud yelp and starts to sob.

"This is quite unbearable!" says his mother, getting up from
the table and throwing down her serviette. "We can never eat
in peace! Your bread sticks in my throat!"

She gestures, dabs her eyes with a handkerchief and leaves
the dining room.

"Now she's offended . . ." mutters Zhilin, forcing a smile.
"She needs some discipline . . . That's how it is, Anfissa Ivanovna, they don't like to hear the truth nowadays . . . I'm
supposed to be the guilty one!"

A few minutes pass in silence. Zhilin looks round at the
plates and notices that no one has touched the soup. He gives
a deep sigh and stares at the flushed and very anxious face of
the governess.

"Why aren't you eating, Varvara Vassilyevna?" he asks. "Offended, are you? There it is. The truth doesn't please . . . So
pardon me, then, my nature is such I can't be a hypocrite. I
cut to the honest truth." He sighs. "However, I see my pres-
ence does not please. When I'm here, you can neither speak
nor eat . . . So what's to be done? You should have told me and
I'd have gone . . . I will go."

Zhilin gets up and walks with dignity towards the door. As
he reaches his weeping son, he stops.

"After all that's been going on here, you're f-f-free," he says,
drawing back his head with dignity. "I won't meddle in your
education any more. I wash my hands of it! I ask pardon because, sincerely like a father, I've disturbed you and your
teachers. So I'm putting aside once and for all my responsibility for what happens to you."

Fedya yelps and sobs more loudly. With dignity Zhilin turns
to the door and goes off to his bedroom.

As he wakes from his after-dinner sleep, Zhilin begins to
feel pangs of conscience. He feels a sense of shame towards
his wife, his son and Anfissa Ivanovna and even a wretched
unease as he remembers what happened during dinner, but his

pride is too great and his courage too small for him to be sincere and so he goes on grumbling and sulking . . .

Waking next morning, he feels in excellent spirits and whistles gaily as he washes. When he goes into the dining room for coffee, he finds Fedya there, who gets up as soon as he sees him and looks at him like someone lost.

"Well, then, young man?" asks Zhilin cheerfully, sitting at the table. "What's the news with you? Still alive, are you? Come here, then, lad, and kiss your father."

Pale and grave-faced, Fedya goes to his father and touches his cheeks with trembling lips, then he goes back and sits silent in his place.

1885

THE EXCLAMATION MARK

❖ ❖ ❖

YEFIM FOMICH PEREKLADIN, A RESPECTED CIVIL SERVANT, went to bed feeling resentful, even thoroughly indignant.

"Oh, stop nagging, you old devil!" he bellowed at his wife, when she asked him why he was so gloomy.

The fact was that he'd just come home from a party where there'd been a lot of talk that jarred on him and made him angry. At first they'd sat there discussing the uses of education in general terms; but then they gradually got on to the educational standard of civil servants, like himself, how very low it was, and distasteful remarks were made, sarcastic quips and even sniggering jokes. And quite soon, as Russians always do when they talk like that, they moved from the general to the downright personal.

A young man had turned to Perekladin and said:

"What about you, Yefim Fomich? You're an example. You've quite a decent position, haven't you, a rank of some importance? What sort of education did *you* have?

"Well, not a great deal," he answered curtly. "But we aren't required to be highly educated, you know. We have to write correctly. That's all there is to it."

"And where were you taught to write correctly, then?"

"Oh, I learned in the usual way, you know. After forty years of service you become an expert. It was quite hard at first, of course. I made mistakes, but then I learned the ropes. And there you are!"

"And what about punctutation marks?"

"Punctuation marks? There's nothing to them. I do them right."

"H'm?" The young man was put off for a moment. "But getting to know the ropes," he went on, "that isn't education, is it? You may well put punctuation marks in the right place. But it's not enough. You have to be conscious of what you're doing. If you put a comma, you should know why. Oh yes! With you it's instinctive. A reflex action. What's the value of that? A mechanical response, that's all."

Perekladin fell silent at this. He even forced a brief smile (for the young man was the son of a counsellor of state and of a certain rank himself) but now, as he tried to sleep, he tossed and turned in indignation.

"Here I've worked for forty years," he thought, "and no one's called me an idiot till now! Then this young fellow comes along! 'Instinctive,' am I? All 'reflex actions' and 'mechanical response.' Oh, go to the devil, you young fool! I understand such things better than you, most likely, even if I haven't been to your universities!"

Cursing his young critic with every curse he knew and warming up under the blankets, Perekladin felt better, calmer.

"I know . . . I understand . . ." he thought, as he was falling asleep, "I don't put a colon where a comma should be, do I, so I know what I'm doing. There you are, young man! Live a little longer, get some experience of work, and then you can criticize an older man . . ."

Across his closed eyes, through a mass of dark and smiling clouds, there flew like a meteor a fiery comma. Behind it came a second and a third, and soon the boundless dark of his imagination was covered by a multitude of flying commas.

"To hell with commas . . ." thought Perekladin, feeling his limbs go luxuriously sluggish as sleep came on. "I know all about them. I'll find a place for every one if you like . . . Knowing what I'm doing too, not at random. Test me and see. Commas go in different places. Sometimes they're essential, sometimes not. The more complicated the document, the more of them you need. They go before 'which' and before 'that.' And if you have a list of officials, you separate them by commas . . . I know!"

The golden commas twirled and spun away. In their place flew fiery full stops.

"And you put full stops at the end . . . And also when you need a breathing space to look up at the listeners. After all long passages you need them so that, when the secretary reads them, he doesn't start stuttering. Full stops go nowhere else at all . . ."

The golden commas came flying back. They tangled with the full stops and whirled about; and Perekladin saw a swarm of semicolons and colons.

"I know those . . ." he thought. "When a comma's not enough and a full stop too much, you need a semicolon. I always put a semicolon before 'but' and 'therefore.' And as for colons? They go after words like 'decided' or 'decreed' . . ."

The colons and semicolons faded. And a row of question marks appeared, leaping out of the clouds and doing the can-can.

"Now there's something: the question mark. Thousands of them, are there? Well, I'll find places for them. You always put them when there's an inquiry or request for information. For example: 'How much remains of the financial account for such and such a year?' Or: 'Cannot the Police Department find, as required, the aforesaid Ivanov?' "

The question marks cast off their hooks in approval and, as if by command, stood straight-backed and became exclamation marks.

"H'm! Now that mark goes very often at the beginning of letters. 'My dear sir!' Or: 'Your excellency, my lord and benefactor!' But where does it go in reports . . . ?"

The exclamation marks stood taller, waiting expectantly.

"They go in reports when . . . it's a matter of . . . When is it now? When, in fact, do you use them? Wait . . . Let me think . . . H'm! . . ."

Perekladin opened his eyes and turned on his other side. But scarcely had he shut them again before the exclamation marks appeared out of darkness.

"Oh, the devil take them! When do you use the things?" he asked himself, trying to drive the unwelcome visitors from his imagination. "Have I actually forgotten? Forgotten . . . or never used them at all . . ."

Perekladin tried to remember all his written work in forty years of service but however much he pondered, however much he frowned, he could not bring to mind from all that time a single exclamation mark.

"Imagine that! I've been a clerk in the civil service for forty years and not once have I put an exclamation mark . . . Where does he go then, that long thin devil?"

From behind the row of fiery exclamation marks there rose up the face of the young man. It smiled spitefully. The fiery marks smiled too, and merged into one huge exclamation mark.

Perekladin shook his head and opened his eyes.

"Oh, the devil!" he thought. "I have to get up early tomorrow and this damned thing won't go out of my head . . . Curse it! But . . . where does it go, then? So much for learning by experience. I've come a cropper. Forty years and not a single exclamation mark! Imagine!"

Perekladin crossed himself and shut his eyes, then opened them immediately: but the huge exclamation mark was there still in the darkness.

"Dash it all, Yefim? Don't you ever go to sleep?"

"Marfusha . . ." Perekladin turned to his wife. Yes, she was always boasting she'd been to a select school for girls. "Tell me something, darling. Do you know when you put exclamation marks?"

"Of course I know. I didn't waste my seven years in a fine school. I know all my grammar by heart. 'Exclamation marks are for salutations, outbursts, and expressions of delight, indignation, joy, anger and similar feelings.' "

"So that's it!" thought Perekladin. "Delight, indignation, joy, anger and similar feelings."

The civil servant began to ponder. For forty years he had written reports, thousands of them, tens of thousands, yet he couldn't recall a single line that expressed delight or indignation or anything of the sort.

"And similar feelings . . ." he wondered. "But what have feelings to do with the work of a civil servant? You write your reports without feelings . . ."

The young man's ugly face peeped again from behind the fiery exclamation mark. It gave another spiteful smile. Perekladin sat up in bed. His head ached and a cold sweat covered his brow . . . A little lamp glimmered softly, the furniture was spick and span, cared for, as it was, by a tender feminine hand, but the poor civil servant felt as chill and comfortless as if typhus afflicted him. The exclamation mark was no longer in the dark behind his eyelids but there before him in the room, near his wife's dressing table. It kept winking at him, full of malice.

"Writing machine!" it whispered like a ghost, "Machine!" and blew cold dry breath all over him. "Insensitive lump!"

The civil servant covered himself with a blanket but under that blanket he still saw the spectre. He thrust his face into his wife's shoulder, but the spectre popped up behind her shoulder.

All night long poor Perekladin suffered, and even with the daylight the spectre did not leave him. He saw it everywhere: in his boots as he put them on, in the saucer of his teacup, on his hanging medal . . .

"And similar feelings . . ." he thought. "It's true. I had no feelings . . . I'll go and report to the Director . . . But what has he to do with feelings? No, that won't do. He's a machine as well: a public relations machine."

When Perekladin went out into the street and called a coachman, it seemed to him than an exclamation mark was driving the vehicle. And the porter in the hall leading to the Director's office looked like an exclamation mark too . . . All things spoke to him of delight, indignation, anger . . . His penholder with the nib also looked like an exclamation mark. Perekladin picked it up, dipped the nib in the ink and wrote his rank and name:

"Collegiate Secretary, Yefim Perekladin!!!"

As he made those three marks, he was delighted, indignant, joyful and burning with anger.

"Take that! Take that!" he muttered, pressing on the pen.

The fiery exclamation mark was satisfied and disappeared.

1885

THE DREAM

❖ ❖ ❖

THERE IS A KIND OF WEATHER WHEN WINTER, AS IF ANGRY AT man's weakness, calls on surly autumn and makes common cause with her. Rain and snow whirl in gloomy fog. A damp, cold, penetrating wind beats spitefully on roofs and windows, roars in pipes and moans in ventilators. Melancholy hovers in the sootlike air. It oppresses nature: damp, cold and frightening.

That was what Christmas Eve was like in 1882, which was before I wore these convict's clothes and worked as a valuer in the money-lender's shop owned by Tupaev, a retired captain.

It was midnight. The storeroom where I spent the night as a sort of watchman was faintly illuminated by a little blue ikon-lamp. It was a big, square room crammed with bundles, trunks and cases. On grey wooden walls through the cracks of which peeped ragged tow, hung coats of rabbit fur, long jackets, guns, pictures, guitars . . . Compelled to watch by night over these goods, I lay on a big red trunk behind the showcase for valuables and stared pensively at the little ikon-lamp.

For some reason I was afraid. The articles there in the money-lender's shop frightened me . . . In the night hours by the ikon's dim light they seemed alive. And now, as rain pattered on the window and wind moaned in the stove, I felt they were making angry sounds. All of them, before they were put there, passed through the valuer's hands, my hands, and so I knew the story of each. For example, the money paid out for that guitar bought medicine for a consumptive's cough ... With that revolver a drunkard shot himself; his wife hid it from the Police, pawned it here and bought his coffin ... The bracelet glinting at me from the showcase was left here by the man who stole it ... Two lace nightdresses, lot 178, were pawned by a girl who needed a rouble for admittance to a Salon where she hoped to ply her trade ... In short, each article told of hopeless grief or sickness, crime or prostitution ...

That Christmas Eve the articles were more persuasive in their pleading.

"Let us go home!" they seemed to moan in the wind. "Do let us!"

But not this alone aroused my feeling of fear. When I leaned over the showcase and cast a timid glance at the dark, misty window, it seemed as if a human face stared from the street into the shop.

"What nonsense!" I pulled myself together. "What foolish fantasy!"

The fact was that I, a valuer for a money-lender, of sensitive nerves, was troubled by conscience that Christmas Eve: a strange thing, even extraordinary. For conscience in the money-lending business is to do with the market, buying and selling, its other features don't apply ... How surprising! Why should they trouble me? I turned from side to side on my hard trunk, screwing up my eyes at the little ikon-light, trying with all my strength to smother this new, unbidden feeling. But my efforts were in vain.

Of course, it was partly physical and moral weariness after long, exhausting work. On Christmas Eve poor people flock in crowds to the money-lenders. Festivals, especially in bitter weather, bring misery to the unfortunate. They come to us for straw and get a stone ... So many brought in things that Christmas Eve that there was no room in the shop and we had to put three-quarters in a shed. With no respite from early morning to late evening I had wrangled with poor folk for groats and copecks, seen their tears and listened to their futile pleading . . . At the end I could scarcely stand on my feet: I was worn out in body and soul. No wonder I couldn't sleep, tossed from side to side and felt frightened . . .

Someone knocked cautiously at my door. Then I heard the voice of my employer.

"Are you asleep, Peter Demyanitch?"

"Not yet. What is it?"

"I think we should open early in the morning, don't you? It's a holiday and the weather's terrible. They'll be swarming here like flies on honey. Don't go out for a meal either, stay in the shop. Good night!"

"That's why I feel afraid," I thought as he went away, "the ikon-lamp keeps flickering. I'll have to put it out."

I got up and went to the corner where the lamp was hanging. The little blue flame guttered weakly as it struggled to keep alive. Each momentary flicker lit ikon, walls, bundles and dark window . . . And in the window two faces were pressed against the pane, peering into the shop.

"There's no one there . . ." I told myself. "I'm imagining it."

And when, having put out the lamp, I was groping back towards my trunk, a little thing happened which was to have no small influence on my later mood . . . Over my head, suddenly and unexpectedly, there sounded for no more than a second a loud squealing whine, as of someone in great pain.

A guitar string had snapped and I, overwhelmed by fear, stuffed my ears and like a madman stumbled over boxes and bundles to my bunk. I buried my head under the pillow and, scarcely breathing, rigid with fear, began to listen.

"Let us go!" the wind and the articles seemed to moan together. "For the sake of this day let us go. You yourself are poor, are you not? You too have known cold and hunger! Let us go!"

Yes, I had been poor and knew what cold and hunger meant. Poverty had forced me to that cursed pawnshop, made me, for a crust of bread, scorn tears and grief. If I were not poor, would I have had the courage to set a price on health, warmth and the pleasures of holiday time? Why did the wind accuse me, my conscience put me on the rack?

But for all the beating of my heart, my fears and pangs of conscience exhaustion claimed her own. I fell asleep. But sleep was shallow . . . I heard my master knocking for me again, the bells for morning service . . . I heard the wind blow and rain beat on the roof . . . My eyes were closed but I saw the things in the shop, the showcase, the dark window, the ikon. The articles crowded round me begging me to let them go home. Whining notes were plucked one after the other on the strings of the guitar, incessantly . . . In at the window peered beggars, old women, prostitutes, waiting for me to redeem their loans, give them back their goods.

I heard through sleep something scratching like a mouse. It scratched a long time, monotonously. I turned and hunched myself up against a cold damp wind blowing fiercely on me. As I pulled a blanket over me, I heard a rustle and a human whisper.

"What a nightmare!" I thought. "Fearful! If only I could wake!"

Some glass fell and broke. A lamp gleamed behind the showcase and light flickered over the ceiling.

"Don't make a noise!" I heard someone whisper. "You'll wake the villain . . . Take your boots off!"

Someone came up to the showcase, looked at me and touched the hanging lock. It was a bearded old man, pale and haggard, in torn soldier's greatcoat and ragged boots. A tall, gaunt fellow followed him, his arms horribly long. He wore a short, tattered jacket and his shirt hung over his trousers. They whispered together and fumbled at the showcase.

"They're stealing!" I realised in a flash.

Though I was asleep, I remembered there was a revolver under my pillow. I silently groped for it and clutched it. The glass of the showcase tinkled.

"Hush! You'll wake him. Then we'll have to kill him."

I dreamt that I screamed wildly from the lungs and, frightened by my own voice, jumped up. The old man and his young companion flung out their arms and fell upon me but, seeing the revolver, drew back. I remember that for a minute they stood in front of me, white-faced, blinking tearfully, pleading with me to let them go. Wind blew fiercely through the broken window and a candle, lit by the thieves, flared up.

"Governor!" said a plaintive voice at the window. "Our benefactor, provider."

I looked at the window and saw an old woman's face, pale, emaciated, dripping with rain.

"Don't hurt them! Let them go!" she wailed, looking at me with pleading eyes. "We are poor!"

"Poor!" repeated the old man.

"Poor!" moaned the wind.

My heart contracted with pain and to force myself awake I braced myself . . . But instead of waking I stood there at the showcase, took things out of it and shoved them jerkily into the pockets of the old man and his companion.

"Take them, quick!" I muttered. "It's Christmas tomorrow and you are beggars. Take them!"

When I'd stuffed their pockets, I made a bundle of the rest of the valuables and flung it at the old woman. Through the window I passed to her a fur coat, a pair of black shoes, a lace nightdress and even the guitar. What a strange dream it was! Then, I remember, the door creaked; and as if they'd sprouted from the ground there stood before me my master, a sergeant and a policeman. My master was nearest but as if I hadn't seen him I went on tying bundles.

"What are you up to, you scoundrel?"

"It's Christmas tomorrow," I said. "They have to eat."

Then a curtain falls. I come to myself and see quite new furnishing. I'm no longer in the money-lender's but in some other place. A policeman comes near me, puts a mug of water by me for the night and mumbles:

"How do you like that? What were you thinking about? And at Christmas too!"

❖ ❖ ❖

When I woke up, it was already light. Rain was no longer beating on the window nor was there moaning wind. Christmas sunshine played cheerfully on the wall. The first to wish me the compliments of the season was the old policeman.

"And a happy housewarming too . . ." he added.

❖ ❖ ❖

A month later they put me on trial. But why? I told the judge it was a dream, that it was unjust to condemn a man for a nightmare. Judge for yourself. Would I for no reason at all hand out other people's goods to thieves and ruffians? And where's the sense in handing them over without a receipt? But the court took dream for reality and condemned me. I'm a convict as you see. Couldn't you, your excellency, put in a good word for me somewhere. I swear by God I'm innocent!

1885

THE MIRROR

❖ ❖ ❖

IT IS NEW YEAR'S EVE. NELLY, THE YOUNG AND ATTRACTIVE daughter of a general, a girl who dreams day and night of marriage, sits alone in her room and looks with weary, half-closed eyes into a mirror. She is pale, tense and as still as the mirror.

An unreal yet seen perspective, like a narrow corridor without end, a row of innumerable candles, the reflection of her face and arms, the mirror's frame—all these have long misted and merged into a shapeless grey sea. The sea undulates, glistens, occasionally glows . . .

It is hard to tell from Nelly's fixed eyes and open mouth whether she sleeps or is awake but all the same she can see. She sees first of all only a smile and a tender, graceful look in someone's eyes, then against the fluid grey appear the shape of a head, a face, brows and a beard. It is he, her husband-to-be, a vision of much longing and hope. He means everything to Nelly: purpose, personal happiness, career and destiny. Without him all things are like that fluid grey: gloom, emptiness, absurdity. No wonder, then, that as she sees the handsome, gently smiling face, she experiences a dream of joy, a rapture not to be put in words. Then she hears his voice, sees how she lives with him under one roof, how her life gradually merges with his. Months pass against the grey . . . years . . . and Nelly, distinctly, in all detail, sees her future.

Picture after picture flickers over greyness. And Nelly sees how on a cold winter's night she raps on the gate of Stepan Loukitch, the doctor. Behind it a lazy old dog barks hoarsely. The windows are dark. All around is silence.

"For God's sake . . . For God's sake!" whispers Nelly.

But then at last the gate creaks and she sees the face of the doctor's cook.

"Is the doctor at home?"

"He's sleeping," the cook whispers into her hands, as if afraid of waking her master. "He's only just come home from the epidemic. I've orders not to wake him."

But Nelly doesn't listen to the cook. Pushing her aside, she runs like a mad thing to the doctor's house. She crosses dark and stuffy rooms, knocking over two or three chairs and at last reaches his bedroom. Stephan Loukitch is lying on the bed, fully dressed except for his coat, and blowing with quivering lips into his palm. A weak night light gleams nearby. Nelly, without a word, sits down and weeps: bitterly, all her body shaking.

"My husband's sick!" she mutters.

Stephan Loukitch does not speak. He slowly rises, props himself up with his fists and peers at her with still and sleepy eyes.

"My husband's sick!" Nelly goes on, controlling her sobbing. "For God's sake, come with me . . . Quickly . . . As quickly as you can!"

"Eh?" mumbles the doctor, blowing on his palm.

"Come with me! At once! Otherwise . . . Otherwise . . . It's terrible to speak of . . . For God's sake!"

And pale and exhausted, gulping back her tears, her breast heaving, Nelly describes her husband's sudden illness and her own inexpressible fear. Her suffering would melt a stone but the doctor peers at her, blows on his palm—and makes no move.

"I'll come tomorrow . . ." he mutters.

"That's out of the question!" cries Nelly in fear. "I know my husband . . . has typhus! Come at once . . . He needs you this minute."

"I've . . . only just got home . . ." mutters the doctor. "For three days I've been fighting an epidemic . . . I'm weary . . . and sick myself . . . It's impossible for me to come. Absolutely impossible . . . I'm infected myself . . . That's how it is!"

And the doctor puts a thermometer before Nelly's eyes.

"My temperature's well over a hundred . . . It's absolutely impossible. I can't even sit up . . . Forgive me . . . I must lie down . . ."

He lies back.

"Doctor, I beg you," moans Nelly in despair. "I implore you. Help me in the name of God. Gather all your strength and come with me . . . I'll pay you, doctor."

"My God! Haven't I already told you? No!"

Nelly jumps up and walks agitatedly about. She wants to explain to the doctor, make him understand . . . It seems to her that if he knows how dear her husband is to her and how unhappy she is, he will forget his exhaustion and his illness. But where can she find the eloquent words?

"Go to the district doctor . . ." she hears him say.

"That's impossible. He lives twenty-five versts away and time is so precious. There aren't enough horses. You're forty versts from where we live and from here to the district doctor's is almost as far . . . No, it's out of the question. Come with me, Stephan Loukitch. I ask a great thing. Oh, please, do it for me. Have pity!"

"The devil know what to . . . I'm burning here . . . Her head's so full of nonsense she doesn't understand . . . I can't help . . . Leave me!"

"But you're obliged to come. You cannot not come! It's selfishness. A man ought to sacrifice his life for his neighbour but you . . . you refuse to turn out! . . . I'll report you to the court!"

Nelly feels that her words are offensive, untrue and undeserved but to save her husband she is ready to forget logic, tact and compassion for others . . . In response to her threat the doctor avidly drinks a glass of cold water. Nelly begins to plead again, begging for pity like the poorest women alive . . . At last the doctor gives in. He slowly gets up, murmuring, struggling for breath, and looks for his coat.

"There it is, your coat!" says Nelly. "Let me help you on with it . . . There you are. Let's go. I'll pay you . . . All my life I'll be grateful . . ."

But then what torment! Once his coat is on, the doctor lies down again. Nelly lifts him and drags him along to the hall. There is a long, agonizing struggle with galoshes and overcoat . . . His cap is missing . . . Then at last Nelly is in the coach, the doctor beside her. Now there are only forty versts to travel and her husband will have medical help. Darkness lies over the land, not a single thing is to be seen. A cold wintry wind blows. The rutted track is frozen under the wheels. The coachman has to stop and consider the way . . .

Nelly and the doctor do not speak to one another through all the journey. They are shaken fearfully about but feel neither that nor the cold.

"Faster! Faster!" Nelly begs the coachman.

At five in the morning the weary horses enter the courtyard. Nelly sees the well-known gates, the well and its tackle, the long row of stables and sheds . . . She is home at last . . .

"Wait, I'll be with you at once . . ." she tells Stepan Loukitch, leaving him on a sofa in the dining room. "Stay there and I'll go and see how he is."

Returning a minute later from her husband, she finds the doctor lying down. He's murmuring something . . .

"Please, doctor . . . I beg you, doctor!"

"What? Ask at Domna's . . ." whispers Stepan Loukitch.

"What?"

"They told you at the meeting. Vlasov said it . . . Who? What?"

And to her great horror Nelly sees that the doctor is as delirious as her husband. What is she to do?

"I'll go to the district doctor!" she decides.

Again there is darkness, the bitter wind, the frozen rutted track. She suffers in body and mind; and there is no ruse of any kind to cheat deceiving nature, ease that suffering . . .

Nelly looks deeper into the greyness and sees how every spring her husband seeks money to pay off the mortgage on their estate. He cannot sleep, nor can she: they think and think till their minds hurt of ways to keep out the bailiffs.

She sees their children. Her endless fear of colds, scarlet fever, diphtheria, bad marks at school, separation. Of their brood of five or six, one dies.

That grey future is not free of death. It is rounded by it. She and her husband cannot die together. One must endure the passing of the other. And Nelly sees her husband die: the terrible event presents itself in every detail. She sees the coffin, the candles, the priest, even the marks the undertaker makes in the hall . . .

"Why? For what reason?" she asks, as she looks, dazed, at the dead face of her husband.

And all the previous life with her husband seems a foolish and unnecessary prelude to this death.

Something falls from her hands and clatters on the floor. She winces, jumps up and opens her eyes wide. A mirror, she sees, is lying at her feet, another stands as it did before on the table. She looks into it and sees a pale, tear-stained face. A grey hinterland is there no longer.

"I must have fallen asleep," she thinks and gives a faint sigh . . .

1885

MISERY

❖ ❖ ❖

"To Whom Shall I Tell My Grief?"

DUSK. Big wet snow-flakes whirling around the just-lit
lamps and settling on roof-tops, backs of horses, shoulders,
caps.

Iona Potapov, sledgeman, is white all over like a ghost. Bent
in on himself as far as living human body can be, he sits on
the box, not moving at all. If all of a snowdrift fell over him,
not even then, you think, would he feel need to shake it off.

His little mare is also white and still; with her stillness, her
angular shape and her straight legs like sticks she has the look
of a gingerbread horse sold for a penny. To all appearances
she's sunk in thought. Any creature dragged from the plow,
from familiar grey landscape and shoved down here, in this
morass of monstrous lights, unceasing roar and rushing people, how can it help but brood . . . ?

Iona and his little mare have not stirred from that spot a
long time now. They came out of the courtyard before dinner
but no fares so far, no fares at all; and now the evening shadows

are gathering over the town, the pale light of the lamps becomes more vivid, the street bustle noisier.

"Sledgeman, to Viborgskaya!" hears Iona. "Sledgeman!"

Iona starts, and through eyelashes plastered with snow sees a soldier in greatcoat and hood.

"To Viborgskaya!" repeats the soldier. "Are you asleep or what? To Viborgskaya!"

To show he is willing Iona clutches the reins, scattering cakes of snow from the mare's back and shoulders.

The soldier sits down in the sledge. The sledgeman clacks his lips, cranes his neck like a swan, rises a little and more from habit than need shakes his whip. The little mare too cranes her neck, crooks her stick-like legs and hesitantly sets off.

"Which way are you pushing, devil?" Iona hears immediate shouts from a dark mass shifting to and fro. 'Where the devil are you going? Keep to the r-right!"

"You don't know how to drive! Keep to the right!" shouts the soldier.

A coachman curses from his coach, a man crossing the road and bumping the mare's nose with his shoulder stares angrily and shakes snow from his sleeve. Iona fidgets on the box as on needles, sticks his elbows into his sides and moves his eyes like a madman as if not knowing where he is or why.

"Such scoundrels, all of them!" jokes the soldier. "Look how they just try to bump into you or fall under the horse's feet. They do it on purpose."

Iona looks at his passenger and moves his lips. He wants to say something, it seems, but only a hoarse noise comes from his throat.

"What?" asks the soldier.

Iona twists his mouth in a smile and croaks, straining his throat:

"Sir, my . . . my son died this week."

"H'm . . . What did he die of?"

"Who can know that? Must be of fever . . . Three days he was in hospital and died . . . God's will."

"Out of the way, devil!" comes out of the darkness. "Gone mad or what, old dog! Use your eyes!"

"Drive on, drive on . . ." says the passenger. "We won't get there till tomorrow at this rate. Get a move on, will you!"

Again the sledgeman cranes his neck, rises a little and swings the whip with clumsy grace. Several times he looks round at the passenger but he has shut his eyes, apparently in no mood to listen.

❖ ❖ ❖

Putting his passenger down at Viborgskaya, Iona stops at a tavern, then sits again, huddled and quite still on the box. Again wet snow plasters him white, the little mare also. An hour passes; another . . .

Along the pavement come three young men stamping galoshes noisily and quarrelling together, two of them tall and thin, the other small and humpbacked.

"Sledgeman, to Police Bridge!" shouts the hunchback in cracked voice. "Three of us . . . Twenty copecks!"

Iona tugs the reins and clacks his lips. Twenty copecks isn't fair rate but payment is no matter to him. A rouble or a five copeck piece, it's all the same to him now if only he has a passenger . . . The young men, pushing and swearing, come to the sledge and all three at once scramble up on the seat. A question faces them: which two will sit, which one stand? After long wrangling, bad temper and abuse they conclude that the hunchback must stand because he is smallest.

"Well then, drive on!" croaks the hunchback, settling into place and breathing down Iona's neck. "Whip away! Well, brother, what a cap you've got! You won't find a worse in all of Petersburg . . ."

"He he . . . He he . . ." laughs Iona. "It's such a one . . ."

"Well then, you, 'Such a one!', drive on! Are you going to go all the way like this? Eh? Want it in the neck?"

"My head's splitting . . ." says one of the tall ones. "Yesterday at Dukmasov's, Vaska and I, we drank four bottles of brandy."

"I can't understand why you tell lies!" The other tall one gets angry. "Lying like a brute!"

"God strike me down! It's true . . ."

"Well, if that's true, then a louse coughs!"

"He he . . ." giggles Iona. "Jo . . . jolly gentlemen!"

"Pah, the devil take you!" snaps the hunchback. "Will you get going, you lump of cholera, or will you not? Is this the way you drive? Slash her with your whip! Oh, the devil, oh! Give her a lovely one!"

Iona feels behind his back the hunchback's fidgeting body and quivering voice. He hears swearing come at him, sees people, and little by little the feeling of loneliness lifts from his chest. The hunchback curses till he chokes on a fancy, treble-barreled oath and bursts out coughing. The tall ones start talking about a certain Nadezhda Petrovna. Iona glances back at them. Then he waits for a brief pause, glances back again and mutters:

"This week my . . . my . . . er . . . son died!"

"We're all going to die . . ." sighs the hunchback, wiping his lips after coughing. "Come on, drive on, drive on! Gentlemen, I just can't put up with crawling like this! When is he going to get us there?"

"Then give him something to cheer him up . . . in the neck!"

"Do you hear, you lump of cholera? I'll make your neck smart. Standing on ceremony with your sort, we might as well walk . . . Do you hear, Snake? Or don't you give a damn what we say?"

And Iona hears more than feels a slap on his neck.

"He he . . ." he laughs. "Jolly gentlemen . . . Your good health!"

"Sledgeman, are you married?" asks one tall one.

"Me, eh? He he . . . Jo . . . jolly gentlemen! The only wife for me these days . . . is the damp earth . . . He ho ho! . . . The grave I mean! . . . There's my son dead and I'm alive . . . Strange business, death mistook the door . . . Instead of coming for me it came for him . . ."

And Iona turns round to tell them how his son died but then the hunchback sighs softly and declares they are there at last, thank God. Iona takes his twenty copecks and stares a long time after the topers, who disappear into a dark doorway. Once more he is alone and once more there is silence for him . . . Misery, calmed a brief time, comes back and tears his heart more cruelly. Anxiously, tormentedly, his eyes searched restlessly the moving crowds on both sides of the street: can't he find a single one at least among these thousands who will listen to him? But the crowds rush by, heeding neither Iona nor his misery . . . Misery is huge, boundless. Let his heart break and misery flow out, then it would flood the whole world so it seems; and yet it is not seen. It is lodged in such an unimportant shell, you couldn't find it with a candle in the daylight . . .

Iona sees the house-porter with a parcel and decides to speak to him.

"Friend, what would the time be?" he asks.

"Ten or so . . . Why've you stopped here, then? Move on."

Iona drives a few paces, cranes over and gives in to misery . . . To speak to people seems to him altogether useless. But not five minutes are gone before he sits up, shakes his head as if he feels sharp pain and tugs the reins . . . He can take no more.

"Back to the yard!" he decides. "Back to the yard!"

And the little mare, as if understanding his thought, begins to trot.

An hour and a half later Iona is sitting by a big dirty stove. On the stove, on the ground and on benches people lie snoring. The air is stuffy and oppressive . . . Iona looks at the sleeping people, scratches himself and is sorry he came home so early . . .

"I've not made enough to pay for the oats," he thinks. "That's why misery's with me. A man who knows his job . . . who eats his fill and so does his horse, he's content all the time . . ."

In one of the corners a young coachman rises, grunts sleepily and reaches for the water-bucket.

"Felt like a drink?" Iona asks him.

"Seemed the way of it, yes!"

"Well, well . . . Good health . . . But my son, brother, he's dead . . . Did you hear? This week, in the hospital . . . What a business!"

Iona watches for the effect of his words but sees nothing. The young man has covered up his head and is asleep already. The old man sighs and scratches . . . As the young man thirsted for water, he thirsts to speak. It will be a week soon since his son died and he has spoken properly of it to no one . . . He must speak about it plainly, deliberately . . . He must tell how his son fell ill, how he suffered, what he said before death came, how he died . . . He must describe the funeral and his visit to the hospital for his dead son's clothes . . . Anisia, his daughter, is still out in the country . . . He must talk about her too . . . Yes, all kinds of things he can talk about now. The one who listens ought to sigh, show sorrow and lament . . . Better still if he spoke to a woman. Yes, they're silly but they start weeping at a couple of words.

"I'll go out and have a look at the mare," thinks Iona. "You've always time to sleep . . . You can sleep, don't worry . . ."

He gets dressed and goes to the stable where the mare is. He thinks about oats, hay and the weather . . . As for his son, when he's alone, he can't think about him . . . To talk about him to someone, that's possible, but to think of him and picture to himself what he was like, it's unbearable anguish . . .

"Munching?" Iona asks his mare as he sees her shining eyes. "Go on, munch, munch . . . If we've not made enough for oats, we'll eat hay . . . Yes . . . I've gotten too old for driving now . . . My son should be driving, not me . . . He was a real sledge-man . . . If only he were alive . . ."

Iona is silent a short time, then goes on:

"That's how it is, mate, my little mare . . . Kuzma Ionitch is gone . . . Departed this life . . . For no reason he went and died . . . Now let's say you had a little foal, and you were its own natural mother . . . And all at once, let's say, this same foal departed this life . . . Wouldn't you be sorry?"

The little mare munches, listens and breathes on her master's hands . . .

Iona is carried away and tells her the whole story . . .

1886

A NIGHT IN THE GRAVEYARD

❖ ❖ ❖

"TELL US A FRIGHTENING STORY, IVAN IVANITCH!"

Ivan Ivanitch twirled his moustache, coughed, smacked his lips, pulled his chair nearer to the young ladies and began:

"My story starts as the best Russian stories generally do: I was, I confess, the worse for drink . . . I had seen in the New Year with an old friend and we'd slobbered about like nobody's business. In my defence I ought to say I didn't get drunk with any pleasure. To mark an occasion like that is quite absurd in my opinion, unworthy of reasonable men. The New Year like the Old is a mess, the only difference is that the Old was bad and the New is even worse . . . We should mark it not, I think, by merry-making but by suffering, tears and plans for suicide. We should remember each New Year that death is nearer, hair sparser, wrinkles thicker, wife older, children bigger and money less . . .

"So I got drunk in grief . . . As I left my friend, the cathedral clock was striking two. The weather was foul: neither autumn nor winter, the devil himself couldn't tell the difference. It was so dark your eyes were blinkered: look where you will, there was nothing to see, as if you were inside a blacking box. Rain thrashed down and cold biting wind made horrible

117

noises: whining, moaning, groaning, screeching as if a witch
had taken over nature's orchestra. Slush slopped sadly under
my feet and lanterns were as dim as weeping widows ...
Nature, it seemed, was sick. It was weather, in short, for ruffians and thieves but not for me, a modest drunken fellow. It
plunged me into a melancholy mood.

" 'Life ...' I mused, as I plashed through mud, '. . . is pale
and empty vegetating ... Illusion ... Day after day, year after
year ... and you're still the same old brute ... More years
to come and still you're just Ivan Ivanitch, drinking, eating,
sleeping ... And in the end they'll bury you, you dolt, eat
funeral cakes at your expense and say: "A good fellow but a
fool unfortunately, didn't leave much money." '

"I was going from Meschanska to Presnya ... quite a distance for a decent drunk ... Struggling on through dark, narrow streets, I didn't meet a living soul nor hear a sound of life.
Afraid of mud getting into my galoshes, I walked first on the
pavement but, for all my precautions, the mud got in and I
moved to the road: less chance there of stumbling on stones
or falling in the gutter. The way ahead was muffled in cold,
thick fog: at first I passed some dimly burning lanterns but
after a street or two even that comfort disappeared. I had to
grope along... Peering into darkness and listening to moaning
wind, I began to hurry ... An inexplicable fear came over me
... It turned to horror when I realised I'd made a mistake and
lost my way ...

" 'Coachman!' I shouted.

"No answer came ... So I decided to move straight ahead,
willy-nilly, hoping that sooner or later I'd come to a main
street where there'd be lights and coachmen. Without turning
my head, afraid to glance aside, I began to run ... Bitter wind
blew against me and thick rain lashed into my eyes ... At
times I was running on the pavement, at others in the street.
How I escaped a broken head after banging into so many pillars
and lampposts I just can't understand."

Ivan Ivanitch drank a glass of vodka, twirled the other half
of his moustache and went on:

"I don't remember how long I ran . . . All I recall is that in the end I stumbled and banged my head against a peculiar object of some sort . . . I couldn't see it but groping at it I had the impression of something cold, wet and smoothly carved . . . I sat on it and rested . . . I don't want to try your patience so I'll only say that after a time, when I struck a match to light a cigarette, I saw that I was sitting on a gravestone . . .

"The sight of that after nothing but mist, not a single human sound, made me shut my eyes and jump to my feet . . . Moving some paces away, I blundered into something else . . . Imagine my horror! It was a wooden cross . . .

'My God,' I thought, 'I've blundered into a graveyard!' I covered my face with my hands and sank down on a gravestone. 'Instead of going to Presnya I've come to Vaganki!'

"I'm not afraid of graveyards or the dead . . . I've no illusions and it's a long time since I took notice of an old wife's tale but there among the silent graves in the dark night and the moaning wind one sombre thought after another came into my head, each worse than the last . . . I felt the hairs bristle on my crown and a coldness from within run over my back . . .

" 'It's not possible!' I consoled myself. 'This is an optical illusion, an hallucination . . . I'm imagining it all . . . under the influence of drink . . . Coward that I am!'

"But just then, as I tried to cheer myself, I heard quiet steps . . . Someone was walking slowly . . . But they were not human steps: they were too quiet, too slight . . .

" 'A dead man . . .' I thought.

Soon this mysterious someone came up to me, touched my knee and sighed . . . Then I heard a wailing . . . It was ghastly, sepulchral, hideous to the spirit . . . If it's frightening for you to hear old women talk of the wailing dead, imagine my feelings as I listened to that sound. I was petrified with horror: not a trace of drunkenness was left . . . It seemed to me that if I opened my eyes and dared to peer into the fog I'd see a face of white and yellow bone, a ragged shroud . . .

" 'Oh God,' I prayed, 'if only it were morning!'

"But before morning I had to endure a horror that defies

description. Sitting on a gravestone and listening to the wailing corpse, I heard other steps ... Something or other was coming straight towards me with heavy, measured tread ... When it reached me, this new ghost from the grave gave a sigh and a moment later a cold bony hand fell heavily on my shoulder ... I lost consciousness."

Ivan Ivanitch drank a glass of vodka and spluttered.

"Well?" asked the young ladies.

"I came to myself in a little square room with dawn's weak light glimmering through a tiny lattice window.

" 'So the dead have dragged me to a crypt ...' I thought.

"Imagine, then, my joy to hear a human voice at the other side of a wall!

" 'Where'd you find him?' it asked gruffly.

" 'Near Belobricov's, monumental masons, your honour ...' another gruff voice replied. 'Where they put their crosses and memorial stones. I saw him sitting there clutching a gravestone with a whining dog beside him ... He must have been drinking ...'

"In the morning, when I woke up again, they sent me away ..."

1886

THE WOLF

❖ ❖ ❖

Nilov, a landowner, thick-set and robust, renowned throughout the district for his remarkable physical strength, and Kyprianov, a detective, returning one evening from hunting, called at old Maxim's mill. Though Nilov's estate was less than a couple of versts away, the hunters felt too tired to go further and decided to rest there for a time. Their decision was also prompted by the fact that Maxim always had tea and sugar, and for hunters kept a decent supply of vodka, cognac and several good things to eat.

After sampling these, the hunters settled down to tea and talk.

"Well, what's the news, old friend?" Nilov asked Maxim.

"What's the news?" The old man grinned. "The news is I'd like to have a gun from you good men."

"And why should you want a gun?"

"Why? Well, I don't need one all that much. I only said that to draw your attention. Shooting's neither here nor there, but who'd have thought a wolf would turn up on my patch? It's the second time he's been prowling about. Yesterday evening near the village he savaged a foal and two dogs, and this morning when it's scarcely light, I go out and there he is, curse him, sitting under a willow tree. Rubbing his snout with his paw. 'Damn you!' I shout at him, and he stares at me like an evil spirit. I fling a stone at him, and he grinds his teeth, his eyes gleam like little candle flames, and he slinks off into a clump of aspens . . . I was scared to death."

"My God!" muttered the detective. "A rabid wolf on the prowl, and we just wandering about . . ."

"Well, what of it?" said Nilov. "We've guns, haven't we?"

"So you'll start shooting at a wolf now?"

"Why shoot him? We can beat him to death with a rifle butt."

And Nilov began to demonstrate that nothing is easier than killing a wolf with a rifle butt and went on to tell how once with a single blow from an ordinary walking stick he felled a mad dog that jumped on him.

"It's easy for you," sighed the detective, looking enviously at his friend's broad shoulders. "You've strength enough for ten, praise God!" Without a stick, even with your fingers you could kill a dog. But as for a simple mortal, while he's lifting the stick and judging where to strike, that dog has time to bite him five times over. It's a nasty business. There's no disease more frightening and horrible than hydrophobia. When I first saw someone suffering from it, I walked about for five days as if I were crazy and I hated every dog-lover and dog in this world. In the first place the suddenness of it all: a man is healthy, calm, he has no cares, and then, out of the blue, a mad dog scratches him. The terrible thought overcomes him there and then, that he is irrecoverably doomed, has no hope of rescue . . . You can imagine, can't you, the agonizing foreboding that stricken man suffers every minute? The disease itself follows the foreboding. And the horrible thing is that it's incurable. Once it shows, it's all up with you. In medicine, as I understand, there's not even the hint of a cure.

"They can cure it in our village, sir," said Maxim. "Miron cured someone completely."

"Rubbish!" sighed Nilov. "All that about Miron is just silly talk. Last summer a mad dog bit Stepka, and Miron and his like could do nothing. They gave him this nasty brew and that, but he went mad and died just the same. No, old friend, at that stage there's nothing to be done. If it happened to me, if a mad dog bit me, I'd put a bullet through my brain."

The chilling talk had an effect. The hunters quietened and drank in silence. Each, despite himself, considered how life and happiness are fatally affected by chance events, things that till then seem of no importance. They became bored and sad.

Nilov finished his tea, stretched himself and got up . . . He wanted to be out in the open. He moved along a row of corn bins, opened a little door and went out. Twilight had already faded into deep evening. The river slumbered.

Over a weir, lit by moonlight, there wasn't a shadow; and in the middle of it the neck of a broken bottle gleamed like a star. Two mill wheels, half in shadow under a broad willow tree, looked sullen and dismal.

Nilov sighed deeply and glanced at the river. Nothing stirred. Bank and water were tranquil, with not even the ripple of a fish . . . But suddenly it seemed to Nilov that along the bank by a clump of osiers something shadowy glided like a dark ball. He peered intensely. The shadow went from sight, then suddenly appeared again, gliding zigzag towards the weir.

"The wolf!" thought Nilov.

But even before the thought came that he must get back into the mill, the dark shape was already on the weir, moving not directly towards him but in zigzag.

"If I run," thought Nilov, "he'll jump on me from behind," and he felt the skin go cold under the hairs of his head. "My God, I haven't even a stick! I must stand my ground . . . and strangle him."

He closely watched the movements of the wolf, judging what each meant. The wolf ran along the weir, almost on a level with him.

"He's going past!" thought Nilov, tensely watching.

But then the wolf, not looking at him and as if reluctant, made a plaintive squeaky sound, turned his face towards Nilov and stood still. He seemed to consider: should he attack Nilov or ignore him?

"Shall I hit him on the head with my fist . . ." thought Nilov, ". . . stun him?"

He was so tense he didn't know who started the fight: himself or the wolf? He only knew that a terrible critical moment had come, when he had to to concentrate all his strength in his right hand and clutch the wolf by the neck. Then something extraordinary happened, hard to believe, seeming like a dream. The wolf howled mournfully and jerked with such force that a layer of its skin, cold and wet, clutched by Nilov's hand, slipped between his fingers. Trying to free its neck, the wolf reared on its back legs, and Nilov grabbed its right paw with his left hand, thrust right up to the socket, then took his right hand from the neck, clutched to the socket of the left paw and lifted the wolf into the air.

It happened in a moment. Then, so that the wolf couldn't bite his arms or turn its head, Nilov thrust the huge fingers of both his hands deep into its neck like spurs. The wolf pushed its paws into Nilov's shoulders and, finding a point of support there, began to struggle with terrible force. It could not bite Nilov's arms and his strong fingers kept its mouth away from his face and shoulders, thrusting and thrusting and causing great pain.

"This is bad!" thought Nilov, stretching back his head as far as possible. "His saliva fell on my lip. I may be done for already, even if, by some miracle, I get out of this."

"Help me!" he shouted. "Maxim! Help me!"

Both of them, Nilov and the wolf, their heads level now, looked each other in the eyes . . . The wolf snapped its teeth, made a squeaky sound and slavered . . . Its back legs, seeking support, knocked against Nilov's knees . . . The moon lit up its eyes, but there was nothing vicious to see there; they seemed to be weeping, like a human being's.

"Help me!" shouted Nilov again. "Maxim!"

But in the mill they did not hear him. Nilov felt instinctively that a great cry would sap his strength, so he didn't shout loudly.

"I'll move back . . ." he decided. "I'll go backwards towards the door, and shout there.

He began to move back, but he hadn't gone two yards when he felt that his right hand was losing strength and beginning to swell. Then came the moment when he heard his own lacerating cry and felt a sharp pain in his right shoulder and something damp and warm running along his arm and chest. Soon he heard Maxim's voice and saw an expression of horror on the detective's face as he ran up.

Nilov let his adversary fall as his fingers sharply parted and he saw that the wolf was dead. Confused by powerful sensations, aware of blood on his thigh and in his right boot, near to fainting, Nilov made his way back to the mill. The sight of the fire and of the samovar and bottles restored his senses, as it were, and brought to his mind the horrors he had just lived through and the danger that was just beginning. Pale, his pupils dilated, his head wet with sweat, he sat on a sack and gave himself up to exhaustion. The detective and Maxim undressed him and began to tend his wound. It seemed serious. The wolf had ripped the skin along the shoulder and even reached the muscles.

"Why didn't you fling him into the river?" asked the white-faced detective, as he staunched the blood. "Into the river, why didn't you fling him there?"

"Stop supposing! My God, no supposing!"

The detective wanted to console and reassure his friend but after his earlier so vivid description of hydrophobia his words would be out of place, so he kept quiet.

Having dressed the wound, he sent Maxim to a nearby farm-house for horses, but Nilov would not wait and went home on foot.

At about six o'clock the next morning, pale and unkempt, haggard from pain and a sleepless night, Nilov arrived at the mill.

"Old friend," he said to Maxim. "Take me to Miron. Hurry! Get in my carriage."

Maxim, also pale after a similar sleepless night, looked about in confusion, then murmured:

"No need to go to Miron, sir . . . I myself, if you'll allow me, know how to cure you."

"All right, then! But hurry, please!"

And he stamped with impatience. The old man set Nilov's face towards the east, muttered something and gave him to drink a mug of unpleasant warm liquid tasting of wormwood.

"But Stepka died . . ." muttered Nilov. "If the people really know a cure, then why did Stepka die? . . . But take me to Miron all the same."

From Miron, in whom he could feel no faith, he called on Ovchinnikov at the local hospital. The doctor gave him belladonna pills and advised him to go to bed. Nilov changed horses and despite terrible pain in his arm drove to the town and to the doctors there.

Some four days later, in the evening, he rushed again to Ovchinnikov and collapsed on his sofa.

"Doctor!" he began, gasping for breath and wiping the sweat from his pale and haggard face! "Grigory Ivanovitch! Do what you like with me, but I can't hold on any longer. Either cure me or poison me, and let's have an end to it! Oh, for God's sake! I'm going out of my mind."

"You ought to take to your bed," said Ovchinnikov.

"To hell with taking to my bed! I'm asking you in plain and simple Russian: what am I to do? You're a doctor. It's your duty to help me! I'm suffering. Every moment, it seems, I'm about to go mad with rabies. I can't sleep, can't eat. The matter's out of my hands now. I've a revolver in my pocket. Every minute I take it out as if to put a bullet through my brain. Grigory Ivanovitch, advise me, for God's sake! What am I to do? Should I see specialists?"

"Very well. Do that if you like!"

"Listen, let's suppose I issue a statement that whoever cures me will receive 50,000 roubles? What do you think of that?

But while it's being printed, there's time for rabies to attack me ten times over. Look, I'm ready to give all I have. Cure me and I'll give you 50,000. Do something for me, in God's name! I don't understand this disgraceful indifference of yours. Do you realise that now I envy every little fly . . . ? I'm miserable. My family is miserable."

Nilov's shoulders quivered, and he burst into tears.

"Now listen, please," said Ovchinnikov, seeking to console him. "I really don't understand why you are hysterical. What are you crying for? Why are you exaggerating the dangers like this? Believe me, you've many more chances of escaping than of falling ill. In the first place, out of every hundred people who are bitten only thirty contract rabies. Then, and this is important, the wolf only bit you through your clothing so the poison would stay there. Even if the poison went into the wound, the flow of blood would wash it out, and you lost a lot of blood. Hydrophobia doesn't worry me in your case, what worries me is the wound itself. In your condition you could contract erysipelas or something similar."

"Is that what you believe? It's true, you're not just consoling me?"

"I give you my word of honour it's true. Look, take this and read it."

Ovchinnikov took a book from a shelf, and then himself began to read to Nilov, omitting alarming sections, a chapter on hydrophobia.

"So it's clear," he concluded, "that you're worrying yourself unnecessarily. And we have to add that neither you nor I know whether the wolf was rabid or not."

"M'm," murmured Nilov and smiled. "At last I understand. My fears were nonsense really."

"Clearly. They were nonsense."

"Oh, thank you, my friend!" Nilov laughed and rubbed his hands with pleasure. "Thanks to you, my clever fellow, oh, I'm so relieved! I'm contented. My God, I'm even happy. I give my word of honour on that . . ."

Nilov put his arms round Ovchinnikov and kissed him three

times. Then there came over him that schoolboy enthusiasm
to which good-natured, physically strong people are prone. He
clutched up a horseshoe from a table and tried to straighten it
out, but he was too weakened by onset of joy and by pain in
his shoulder to be able to do it. He contented himself with
clasping the doctor below the waist with his left hand, lifting
him and carrying him over his shoulder from the surgery into
the dining room.

He went out from Ovchinnikov in high good humour, and
it even seemed that the little tears glistening on his broad
black beard were cheerful as he was. As he descended the
steps, he laughed in a deep bass voice and shook the hand-rail
so violently that a baluster dropped out and all the verandah
shuddered under Ovchinnikov's feet.

"What a Hercules!" thought Ovchinnikov, looking affec-
tionately at his broad back. "What a boy he is!"

As he settled in his carriage, Nilov began to relate from the
very beginning in great detail how he fought a wolf on a weir.

"It was a game!" he concluded, laughing happily. "Something to remember in my old age. Come on, coachman, speed
up!"

1886

THE TRICK

❖ ❖ ❖

Aclear winter noon . . .

A frost, hard and crackling, and Nadenka, holding me under the arm, had silver rime on curls at her temples and the down of her upper lip. We stood on a high hill and from our feet a slope, reflecting the sun like a mirror, stretched all the way down. Beside us was a little sledge upholstered in bright red cloth.

"Let's slide down, Nadejda Petrovna," I pleaded. "Just once. I assure you, we'll come through safe and sound."

But Nadenka was afraid. All the way down from her tiny galoshes to the bottom of the icy slope seemed a terrifying abyss, immeasurably deep. Her heart sank and her breathing stopped when she looked down or when I merely suggested sitting in the sledge. If she took a risk and hurtled into the abyss, what then? She'd die, lose her senses.

"I beg you," I said. "There's no need to be afraid. That's mean-spirited, you know, cowardice!"

At last Nadenka gave in and I saw from her face that she did it with fear for her life. I seated her, pale and trembling, in the sledge, clutched her hand and down we sped together into the abyss.

The sledge flew like a bullet. The cleaving air whipped, howling, into our faces, whistled in our ears, tore and tweaked at us in hurtful spite and tried to rive the heads from our shoulders. The wind's force took away our power to breathe. It was as if the devil himself had clutched us in his claws and with a roar was rushing us to hell. Everything about us blurred together in a single, headlong-rushing strip. Only a moment more, it seemed, and we would perish!

"I love you, Nadia!" I whispered.

The sledge began to move more quietly, more quietly, the roar of wind and the whirr of runners less fierce, we were free to breathe again and there we were, at last, at the bottom. Nadenka seemed neither alive nor dead. She was white, scarcely breathing . . . I helped her up.

"I'll not go again for anything," she said, looking at me with wide eyes full of horror. "Not for anything on earth! I nearly died!"

After a little time she recovered and looked inquiringly into my eyes: had I said those four words or did she only seem to hear them in the wind? And I stood beside her, smoking, and carefully examining my glove.

She took me by the arm and for a long time we walked about the hill. Clearly the puzzling question gave her no peace. Were those words spoken or weren't they? Yes or no? Yes or no? It was a matter of pride, of honour, of life and happiness, of great consequence, the greatest on earth. Impatiently, sadly and with a searching expression, Nadenka looked into my face, responding absent-mindedly as she waited, wondering if I'd speak. Oh, what a play of expression on that dear face, what indeed! I saw her struggle with herself; she had to say something, ask a certain question but couldn't find words, was ill at ease, alarmed, disturbed by joy . . .

"Do you know something?" she said, not looking at me.

"What?" I asked.

"Let's do it once more . . . slide down."

We climbed the steps to the hill top. Again I seated Nadenka, pale and trembling, in the sledge and again we hurtled down into the terrifying abyss; the wind roared again and the runners whirred, and again, when noise and speed were fiercest, I whispered:

"I love you, Nadia!"

As the sledge came to a halt, Nadenka glanced back at the hill we'd sped down and then looked a long time into my face and listened intently to my indifferent and impassive voice; and everything about her, even her muff and hood, all of her figure expressed extreme bewilderment.

Her face was saying: "What on earth was it? Who pronounced *those* words? Did he, or did I only seem to hear them?"

The uncertainty made her agitated, put her quite out of patience. The poor girl made no reply to questions and she frowned, on the edge of tears.

"Shall we go home?" I asked.

"But ... but I like tobogganing ..." she said, blushing. "Shall we go once again?"

She "liked" tobogganing: all the same, sitting in the sledge, she was pale and trembling, just as before, could scarcely breathe for fear.

We went down for the third time and I saw how she looked into my face, watching my lips. But I put a handkerchief to my lips and coughed, and when we were half way down, I managed to murmur:

"I love you, Nadia!"

And so the enigma was enigma still. Nadenka was silent, preoccupied ...

I saw her home from the rink. She endeavoured to move more quietly, slowing her steps and never ceasing to wonder whether I'd speak those words. And I saw how her spirit was troubled and what control she had to exercise to keep from saying:

"It can't really be the wind that spoke those words. And I don't want it to be the wind!"

Next morning I received a note: "If you're going today to the rink, then call for me. N."

And from then on I began to go there with Nadenka every day and every time we hurtled down in the sledge I whispered the very same words:

"I love you, Nadia!"

Quickly Nadenka became addicted to the words as if to wine or morphia. She couldn't live without them. It was true that hurtling down the slope was terrifying from the very first but fear and danger gave peculiar force to fascinating words of love which from the very first remained a strange enigma troubling her soul. There were only two suspects indeed: the wind and I. Which of them confessed their love she did not know, but clearly it was all the same to her. This drinking cup or that, it's all the same if only you get drunk.

For some reason once at midday I went to the rink. Mingling with a crowd, I saw Nadenka go to the hill as if she were looking for me . . . Then she went timidly up the steps. She was afraid to slide down alone, so afraid. She was white as snow and trembled as if she were going to execution. But go she did, her mind made up, without a backward glance.

Clearly she had decided at last to make the test: would she hear those wonderfully sweet words if I were not there?

I saw how, blanching, mouth wide with horror, she sat in the sledge, closed her eyes and with a last farewell to earth set off.

"Zzzzzz . . ." zoomed the runners. Whether Nadenka heard the words I do not know. I only saw how weak and exhausted she was as she got out of the sledge. And her face showed clearly that she herself did not know if she heard anything or not. Her fear as she swept down took away her power to hear, to distinguish sounds and understand . . .

But then March was upon us and spring. The sun grew warmer, our icy slope darkened, losing its sheen and finally melted away. We stopped tobogganing. There was nowhere anymore for poor Nadenka to hear those words, nor anyone to say them either, for the wind was silent and I was going to Petersburg, for a long time, perhaps forever.

It happened that before I left, a couple of days before, I was sitting at twilight in a little garden separated from the place where Nadenka lived by a high nailed fence. It was cold enough still, snow still about by the muck heap and the trees dead; but spring was in the air for all that, and rooks cawed loudly as they settled to their nests at nightfall. I went up to the fence and looked a long time through a crack . . .

I watched as Nadenka came out on the porch and turned a mournful, yearning glance at the sky . . . The spring wind blew straight into her pale, dejected face . . . It reminded her of the wind that roared at us on the slope when she heard those four words, and her face went sad, most sad, a tear running on her cheek . . . And the poor girl stretched out both arms as if imploring the wind to bring those words again. And with the wind I whispered:

"I love you, Nadia!"

My God, the effect on her! She cried out, smiled with all her face and stretched her arms into the wind, delighted, joyful, so beautiful.

And I went to pack . . .

That was all a long time ago. Nadenka is married now: they gave her or she gave herself—it's all the same—to a secretary for wardship of estates and she has three children already. But she hasn't forgotten how she went with me to the rink and how the wind carried the words, "I love you, Nadia!" It is now the happiest, most endearing and beautiful memory of her life . . .

And now, as I've grown older, I really don't know why I said those words, for what reason I played the trick.

1886

AGAFYA

❖ ❖ ❖

During my stay in the district of S—, I often went to the Dubovsk allotments to see Savva Stukatch, or simply Savka. Those allotments were my favourite place for so-called "common or garden fishing," when you leave home, not knowing the day or hour you'll come back, taking all your tackle at once and all the food you need. In actual fact, the fishing didn't attract me as much as the carefree lazing about, eating when I felt like it, the chats with Savka and long contemplation of the quiet summer nights.

Savka was a young chap of twenty-five, big, handsome and rugged as flint. People thought he had common sense and was intelligent, he could read and write and rarely drank, but as a workman, though young and strong, he wasn't worth a brass farthing. For all his powerful muscles, strong as cord, a heavy, irremoveable laziness pervaded him. He lived, like all the other peasants, in the village and had his own cottage and his own plot of land, but he neither ploughed nor sowed nor had a trade. His old mother begged from door to door but he lived like a bird in the sky, not knowing in the morning what he'd eat at noon. It wasn't that he lacked will-power or energy or had no pity for his mother, but simply that he felt no desire to work nor did he see the need for it . . .

All his figure breathed a serene, intuitive, almost artistic passion for living carelessly, taking it easy. But when his young healthy body had a physical need for muscular work, he'd casually take up some foolish occupation like sharpening unwanted stakes or running races with peasant women. His favourite stance was one of concentrated stillness. He could stand for hours in one place without stirring, his eyes on a particular spot. He moved on impulse and then only when a quick, impetuous action of some kind was needed, such as catching a dog by the tail, tearing off a woman's kerchief or jumping over a big hole in the ground. Clearly because he was so loath to move, Savka was as poor as a falcon in the sky and lived worse than a tramp. In time, of course, his debts accumulated and the village council gave him an old man's job, watchman and scarecrow at the allotments. Though they mocked him for his premature old age, it went in one ear and out the other. This quiet place, ideal for stillness and contemplation, quite suited his nature.

I happened to be with Savka one lovely May evening. I was lying, I remember, on a torn, bedraggled rug just by the hut from which came a dense, sultry smell of dried herbs. I put my hands behind my head and looked forward. At my feet lay a wooden pitchfork. Behind it, like a dark stain, I could see Kutka, Savka's dog, and no more than twelve feet beyond the earth fell in a steep bank to the river. I couldn't see the river from where I lay. I saw only the tops of a thick clump of willows on this side and the edge of the opposite bank twisting in, as if gnawed away. Far off, beyond the bank, on a dark little hill, clustered together like frightened young partridges, were the huts of the village where Savka lived. Behind the hill was the light of the setting sun. All that remained was a pale crimson strip and even that was beginning to be covered by little clouds like ash on a fire.

To the right of the allotments, whispering softly and occasionally shuddering in gusts of wind, was a dark copse of alder-trees; and to the left stretched an endless plain. There where in darkness the eye could not distinguish plain from sky, a light glimmered brightly.

Savka sat at a little distance from me. His feet tucked under him, Turkish fashion, his head drooping, he looked pensively at Kutka. Our hooks with live bait had been set in the river a time ago and there was nothing to do but enjoy taking it easy, which Savka, never tired and always at ease, loved so much. Twilight had not quite died away but summer night already folded nature in a soothing caress.

All things sank into their first sleep except some bird of the night, unknown to me, that lazily gave a long, articulated cry, sounding like "You saw Ni-ki-ta?" and then seemed to reply: "I saw him! I saw him! I saw him!"

"Why aren't the nightingales singing tonight?" I asked Savka.

He slowly turned towards me. His features were large but as clear, expressive and soft as a woman's. Then he glanced with gentle, dreamy eyes at the copse and the willows, slowly took a whistle from his pocket, put it in his mouth and whistled the notes of a hen-nightingale. At once, as if in reply to his call, a corncrake clacked.

"There's a nightingale for you," laughed Savka. "Jerk! Jerk! As if he's jerking at a hook, and I bet he thinks he can sing too."

"I like that bird," I said. "Do you know, corncrakes don't fly when they're migrating, they run along the ground. They only fly over rivers and seas, otherwise they're on foot."

"Fancy that, the rogues . . ." muttered Savka with a respectful glance where the corncrake was calling.

Knowing how much Savka liked listening to talk, I told him all I knew from hunting books about the corncrake. From that I moved imperceptibly moved to migration. Savka listened attentively, without a blink, smiling all the time in pleasure.

"And where are the birds most at home?" he asked. "With us or over there?"

"With us, of course. The birds grow up here and hatch their

young, this is their native place, they only fly away there so
as not to freeze to death."

"Interesting!" drawled Savka. "Talk of anything, it's interesting. That bird now, or man . . . Or take that little stone . . .
They all have things to be known . . . Ah, if I'd known you
were coming, sir, I wouldn't have asked that woman over here.
She pestered me to come today . . ."

"Oh, please, I mustn't be in your way," I said. "I can go and
lie down in the copse."

"Oh no, let it be! She wouldn't have died if she came tomorrow . . . If only she'd sit and listen to the talk . . . but she'd
start slobbering. You can't talk sensibly when she's here."

"Is it Darya you're expecting?" I asked after a pause.

"No. A new one this time and very keen . . . Agafya, the
signalman's wife . . ."

Savka said this with his usual, passionless, rather husky
voice, as if talking of tobacco or cabbage, and I started with
surprise. I knew Agafya, the signalman's wife . . . She was a
quite young peasant girl of nineteen or twenty who had been
married only about a year to a lively young fellow. She lived
in the village and her husband came home to her every night
from the railway.

"These affairs you have with women will turn out badly,"
I said with a sigh.

"Let them . . ."

Then, thinking a moment, Savka added:

"I've told the women, they don't listen . . . Don't give a
damn, the fools!"

There was a silence . . . Meanwhile darkness thickened and
things lost their outline. The thread of light behind the hill
had altogether faded and the stars became clearer and more
luminous . . . The melancholy, repetitive chirr of grasshop-
pers, the grating of the corncrake and the cries of quail did
not disturb the silence of night but rather gave it a deeper
monotony. It seemed that it was not birds nor insects that
made soft noises charming the ear but the stars looking down
from the sky . . .

It was Savka who broke the silence. He slowly turned his eyes from his black dog and said:

"I see you're bored, sir. Let's have supper."

And, not waiting for my agreement, he crawled on his stomach into the hut, rummaged about there so that it all quivered like a big leaf, and then crawled back and put my bottle of vodka and an earthenware bowl in front of me. In the bowl were hard-boiled eggs, rye cakes, fried in lard, pieces of black bread and a few other things . . . We drank from a crooked, wobbly glass and began to eat . . . Coarse grey salt, dirty, greasy cakes, rubbery hard-boiled eggs, but all the same how tasty it was!

"You live like a lonely peasant but look at the good things you have!" I pointed to the bowl. "Where did you get them?"

"The women bring them . . ." mumbled Savka.

"What do they bring them for?"

"Well . . . Out of pity . . ."

Not only the food but Savka's clothes too showed traces of the "pity" of women. I noticed that evening he had a new belt of worsted yarn and a bright crimson ribbon from which a little copper cross hung over his dirty neck. I knew the fair sex's weakness for Savka and how reluctant he was to talk about it, so I did not go on with my questioning. And, in fact, there wasn't time for talking. Kutka, who had been pining near us, patiently waiting for scraps, suddenly pricked up her ears and growled. We heard a distant, intermittent splashing.

"Somebody's crossing the ford," said Savka.

Three minutes later Kutka growled again and made a noise like a cough.

"Shut up!" her master shouted.

Timid footsteps sounded dully in the darkness and the figure of a woman came out of the copse. I recognized her in spite of the darkness. It was Agafya, the signalman's wife. She came hesitantly towards us, stopped and panted. She was breathless not so much from walking probably as from fear and the unpleasant feeling we all have crossing a ford at night. Seeing two men by the hut instead of one, she gave a weak cry and stepped back a pace.

"Oh, it's you!" said Savka, stuffing a cake in his mouth.

"Me . . . Yes, me . . ." she muttered, dropping a bundle of something on the ground and casting a sidelong glance in my direction. "Yakov sends you his regards and asks me to give you . . . this thing here . . ."

"That's a lie, that is: Yakov!" Savka grinned. "No need to lie, the gentleman knows why you've come. Sit down and eat with us."

Agafya looked askance at me and hesitantly sat down.

"I was beginning to think you weren't coming tonight," said Savka after a prolonged pause. "What are you sitting there for? Eat! Or are you after a drop of vodka?"

"Fancy!" said Agafya. "Do you take me for a drunkard?"

"Drink anyway . . . It'll cheer you up, won't it!"

Savka gave Agafya the wobbly glass. She slowly drank the vodka, eating nothing with it, and noisily blowing out her breath.

"You've brought something . . ." Savka went on, undoing the bundle and giving a condescending, teasing tone to his voice. "Women just can't come here without bringing me things. Ah, a pie and potatoes . . . They live well!" He sighed, turning his face to me. "In the whole village they're the only ones left with potatoes in the winter!"

In the darkness I didn't see Agafya's face but from the movements of her shoulders and head it seemed to me she couldn't keep her eyes from Savka's face. Not wanting to be the odd man out, I decided to go for a walk and got up. But just then a nightingale in the grove sang suddenly two low contralto notes. Half a minute later it gave a fine high trill and, having tested its voice, began to sing. Savka jumped up and listened.

"It's the one from last night," he said. "Just wait!"

And he darted off silently into the grove.

"Eh, why are you going after him?" I shouted. "Wait!"

Savka waved his hand, meaning, "Don't shout, then," and disappeared into the darkness. When he wished, Savka was a splendid hunter and fisherman but these talents ran to waste like his strength. He was too lazy for the necessary routine methods and wasted his passion for hunting in futile tricks. He would always try to catch nightingales with his hands, shoot pike with a shotgun or stand for hours at a river bank to catch little fish with a big hook.

Left with me, Agafya coughed and rubbed the palm of her hand several times across her forehead. She was becoming tipsy with the vodka.

"How are things, Agafya?" I asked after a long silence that was becoming awkward.

"All right, thank God . . . But you won't tell anyone, sir, will you?" she added in a sudden whisper.

"Yes, to be sure." I calmed her. "But what a risk you're taking, Agafya . . . What if Yakov finds out?"

"He won't . . ."

"But what if he does?"

"No . . . I'll be home before him. He's working on the line now and he'll come back with the mail train, and we'll hear when it's coming . . ."

Agafya rubbed her brow again with her hand and looked where Savka had gone. The nightingale sang. Some night bird flew low just over the earth and noticing us, fluttered its wings and flew across the river.

Soon the nightingale was silent but Savka did not come back. Agafya got up, made a few restless paces and sat down again.

"What's he doing, then?" She was unable to restrain herself. "The train won't be running tomorrow. I'll have to be going soon."

"Savka!" I shouted. "Savka!"

Not even an echo answered. Agafya stirred uneasily and got up again.

"It's time for me to go," she said in agitated voice. "The train will be here directly. I know when they come."

The poor girl was not mistaken. Not a quarter of an hour had passed when a distant rumble was heard.

Agafya stared at the copse for a long time and impatiently
moved her arms.

"Well, where is he, then?" she said, laughing nervously.
"Where the devil has he got to? I'm going, sir. Oh God, I'll
have to go."

Meanwhile the noise of the train was becoming clearer. You
could distinguish the rumble of the wheels from the chuffing
of the engine. Then a whistle sounded, the train jolted dully
across a bridge . . . and a minute later all was silent.

"I'll wait another minute . . ." Agafya sighed, determinedly
sitting down. "So be it! I'll wait!"

At last Savka appeared out of the darkness. He walked noiselessly in bare feet over the loose earth of the allotment, hum-
ming softly to himself.

"What luck, do me a favour!" He laughed cheerfully. "As
soon as I got to the bush, I tell you, and got my hands ready,
he went silent. Dirty dog! I waited, waited for him to start
again, but I had to pack it in . . ."

Savka sank clumsily to the ground near Agafya and to keep
his balance clutched at her waist with both hands.

"What are you looking like a cross baby for?" he asked.

For all his kindness and good nature Savka despised women.
He treated them carelessly, condescendingly, and even
laughed scornfully at their feelings for him. God knows, perhaps this careless, scornful treatment was one reason why he
strongly and irresistibly attracted the village Dulcineas. He
was handsome and well-built and there always gleamed a soft
tenderness in his eyes, even as he looked at the women he so
despised, but you can't explain his fascination by one quality
alone. Apart from his contented look and peculiar ways, I
suppose the women were also attracted by his touching role
of a recognized failure, exiled from his native village to the
allotment.

"Well, tell the gentleman what you came here for?" Savka
went on, still holding her by the waist. "Come on, then, married woman! Ho ho! A drop more vodka for you, is it, Agasha,
mate o' mine?"

I got up and, making my way between ridges of earth, went along the edge of the allotments. The dark ridges looked like big flattened graves. They had a smell of dug-up earth and the tender damp of plants beginning to be covered with dew . . . To the left the red light still gleamed. It twinkled cheerfully, as if smiling.

I heard a happy laugh. It was Agafya.

"But the train?" I remembered. "It arrived long ago."

After waiting a little I went back to the hut. Savka sat cross-legged and motionless like a Turk and quietly, scarcely heard, hummed a song of what seemed monosyllables, rather like: "Oo—you—you—you . . . me—and—you . . ." Agafya, intoxicated by vodka, Savka's scornful caresses and the stifling night, lay by him on the earth, her face pressed convulsively to his knee. So deeply absorbed, she did not even notice my arrival.

"Agasha, the train's been here a long time," I said.

"Time, time for you to go," said Savka, as he understood what I meant and shook his head. "What are you sprawling for, you hussy?"

Agafya started, lifted her head from his knee and looked at me, then sank to him again.

"It's long been time," I said.

She turned and got up on one knee. She was suffering. For half a minute her whole figure, as far as I could judge in darkness, expressed vibrant conflict. For a moment, as if coming to, she stretched her body to get up, but some invincible and implacable force thrust her back and she clung to Savka.

"Damn him!" she said with a wild laugh deep in her throat in which reckless determination, weakness and pain were all heard.

I strolled quietly to the copse and from there went down to the river where our fishing tackle was. The river was asleep. A soft, double-headed flower on a high stalk tenderly touched my cheek like a child wanting to let you know he's not sleeping. Having nothing to do, I felt at a line and pulled it . . . It strained weakly and hung limp: nothing was caught . . . I couldn't see the opposite bank and the village. A light twinkled in one of the huts but soon went out. I felt along the bank, found a hollow I had noticed during the day and sat in it like an armchair. I sat there a long time . . . I saw the stars mist over and lose their radiance and felt the cool of evening pass like a light sigh over the earth, stirring the slumbering willow leaves.

"A—gaf—ya!" came a dull voice from the village. "Agafya!" The anxious husband had returned to the village and was looking for his wife. And just then irrepressible laughter sounded from the allotments: his wife, forgetting everything and intoxicated by a few hours of happiness, was trying to make up for the torment awaiting her next day.

I fell asleep . . .

When I awoke, Savka was sitting by me and shaking me lightly by the shoulder. River, both banks green and washed with dew, copse, trees and fields—all were bathed in bright morning light. Through the thin trunks of the trees the rays of the risen sun beat on my back.

"So that's how you catch fish?" laughed Savka. "Come on, get up!"

I got up, stretched luxuriously, and drank in moist, fragrant air.

"Has Agafya gone?" I asked.

"There she is!" said Savka and pointed towards the ford. I looked and saw Agafya. Holding up her skirt, dishevelled, her kerchief slipping from her head, she was crossing the river. Her legs were moving scarcely at all . . .

"The little cat knows whose meat she's had a taste of!" muttered Savka, screwing up his eyes as he looked at her. "There she goes, tail between her legs . . . Lecherous as cats these women and frightened as hares . . . She wouldn't go last night, the fool, when we told her . . . Now she's going to catch it . . . and I'll be up before the district court . . . Another flogging on account of women . . ."

Agafya stepped on the bank and went across the fields to the village. At first she walked boldly enough but soon fear

and agitation gripped her: she turned back in fright, stopped
to draw breath.

"Ay, she's scared!" Savka laughed sadly, looking at the
bright green streak she had made across the dewy grass. "She
doesn't want to go! Her husband's been standing there waiting
a full hour . . . Have you seen him?"

Savka spoke the last words with a smile but I had a chill
feeling under the heart. At the far end of the village near his
hut Yakov was standing, staring at his wife as she came back
to him. He made no movement, was still as a post. What was
he thinking as he looked at her? What words was he preparing
for their meeting? Agafya stopped a moment, looked back once
more as if expecting help from us, then went forward. I never
saw anyone, drunk or sober, move in the way she did. It was
as if Agafya was flung into writhing by her husband's gaze.
She zigzagged or trampled on one spot, giving way at the knees
and flinging her arms about, or went backwards. After about
a hundred paces of it she turned back once again and sat down.

"You ought at least to hide behind a bush . . ." I told Savka.
"Or her husband will see you . . ."

"He knows without that who Agasha's been with . . .
Women don't go to the allotments at night just for cabbages.
Everybody knows."

I looked at Savka's face. It was pale and twisted with the
disgust and pity of those who see animals being hurt.

"The cat laughs, the mouse cries," he said.

Agafya suddenly jumped up, tossed her head and walked
boldly to her husband. Clearly she had plucked up her courage,
made up her mind.

1886

A Gentleman Friend

❖ ❖ ❖

The lovely Vanda, or, as she was named in her passport, Citizen Nastasia Kanavkina, was discharged from hospital and found herself in a situation she had never known before: with nowhere to go and not a copek to call her own. What was she to do?

She went first of all to the pawnbroker's and put in pawn her turquoise ring—her only jewel. They gave her a rouble for it . . . but what can you buy with a rouble? Not a smart jacket anyway, nor a high hat, nor brown shoes, and without them she felt quite naked. It was as if not only people, but even horses and dogs, were looking at her and laughing at her shoddy clothes. It was her clothes she kept thinking about: what she was going to eat and where she'd spend the night didn't worry her.

"If only I could meet a gentleman friend . . ." she thought, "I'd get some money. There isn't one who would refuse me, because, you see . . ."

But she didn't meet a gentleman friend. It wouldn't have been difficult to meet one in the evening at the "Renaissance," but they wouldn't let her in there in her shoddy clothes and

without a hat. What was she to do? After long hesitation, tired
of walking or sitting and thinking, Vanda decided to try a last
resort: to call on a gentleman friend at his house and ask for
money.

"But which one shall I go to?" she wondered. "Not to Misha,
oh no! He's with his family . . . And that red-haired old fellow
will be at work . . ."

Then Vanda remembered Finkel, the dentist, a Jew who'd
become a Christian. He gave her a bracelet three months ago,
and once at supper in the German club she poured a glass of
beer over his head. Remembering Finkel like that cheered her
up no end.

"He's sure to give me something," she thought, as she set
off. "If I find him at home, that is. And if he doesn't, I'll smash
every lamp in the house."

When she came to the dentist's door, she had a plan ready:
she'd run laughing up the stairs, dash into his surgery and ask
him for twenty-five roubles. But as she was about to ring the
bell, the plan, as if of itself, went clean out of her head; and
Vanda suddenly felt ashamed and agitated in a way she had
never felt before. She could be bold and cheeky as you like in
a group of drinkers: but now, wearing a dreary dress, a humble
petitioner likely to be rejected, she was timid and meek. She
became ashamed and scared.

"He may even have forgotten all about me," she thought,
reluctant to pull the bell. "And how can I go to him in this
dress? Like a beggar-woman or a dowdy working girl . . ."

And hesitatingly she rang the bell.

She heard steps and the doorman appeared.

"Is the dentist in?" she asked.

She would have felt happier if the doorman had said no, but
without replying he led her into the hall and took her coat.
The staircase seemed luxurious to her, magnificent, but from
all its splendour the first thing to meet her eyes was a big
mirror, in which she saw a shabby woman with neither a
high hat, nor a smart blouse, nor brown shoes. And it seemed

strange to Vanda that now, when she was shabby and looked like a seamstress or a washerwoman, a shame came over her and she lost her impudence and daring and in her thoughts she was no longer Vanda but, as in earlier days, Nastasia Kanavkina.

"This way, please," said a servant girl, leading her into the surgery. "The dentist will be here in a moment. Sit down."

Vanda sank into a soft chair.

"So I'll say this to him: lend me some money, please!" she thought. "It will be all right because he knows me. If only that girl would go away. It's hard with her watching . . . Why is she standing there?"

Five minutes later the door opened and Finkel came in, a tall, swarthy Jew with fleshy cheeks and bulging eyes. His cheeks, his eyes, his belly, his plump thighs—all of him—seemed well-fed, gross and stern. In the Renaissance and the German Club he was jolly most of the time, spent money on the ladies and patiently put up with their pranks (and when for instance, Vanda poured beer over his head, he only smiled and wagged a finger at her); but now he had a frowning, sluggish face, looked about him seriously and coldly like a master and went on chewing something.

"What can I do for you?" he asked, with scarcely a glance at Vanda.

Vanda looked at the serious face of the servant girl and at the well-fed figure of Finkel who didn't seem to recognize her, and she blushed.

"What can I do for you?" repeated the dentist, becoming irritated.

"Oh . . . my teeth hurt . . ." whispered Vanda.

"Ah ah . . . Which teeth? . . . Where?"

Vanda remembered she had one tooth with a hole in it.

"Down there . . . On the right . . ." she said.

"Ah! . . . Open your mouth."

Finkel frowned, seemed to hold his breath and began to examine the tooth.

"Does it hurt?" he asked, probing the tooth with a metal thing.

"Yes, it does," lied Vanda.

"I should remind him," she thought, "so that he recognizes me. But . . . that servant girl! Why is she standing there?"

Finkel snorted suddenly like a steam engine straight into her mouth and said:

"I don't advise a filling. That tooth's no use to you at all."

Probing the tooth again and smearing Vanda's lips and gums with his tobacco-stained fingers, he drew in his breath again and pushed something cold into her mouth . . . Vanda felt a sudden sharp pain, shrieked and clutched Finkel's arm.

"Never mind, never mind!" he muttered. "Don't be afraid . . . The tooth's no use to you. You must be brave."

And then his fingers, stained with tobacco and blood, held up before her eyes the tooth he had pulled out, while the servant girl came up and put a cup to her lips.

"Rinse your mouth out with cold water when you get home," said Finkel. "That'll stop the blood."

He stood in front of her, as if expecting her to go and leave him in peace.

"Goodbye," she said and turned towards the door.

"Hum! . . . And who is going to pay me for my work?" asked Finkel in an amused voice.

"Oh yes." Vanda remembered she had to pay, blushed and gave him the rouble she got for her turquoise ring.

Going out into the street, she felt even more ashamed than before, but this time it wasn't her poverty she was ashamed of. She no longer noticed she hadn't a high hat nor a smart jacket. She went along, spitting blood, and each red drop spoke of her life, her hard and wretched life, of the humiliations she suffered and would suffer tomorrow, in a week, in a year—all her life till death came.

"Oh, how awful it is!" she whispered. "My God, it's horrible!"

Nevertheless she was at the Renaissance the following day, dancing there. She wore a huge red hat, a smart jacket and brown shoes. For a young merchant from Kazan was treating her to supper.

1886

Love Affair with a Double-Bass

❖ ❖ ❖

Sмichkov, the musician, was on his way from town to Prince Bibulov's *dacha*, where, to celebrate a betrothal, an evening of music and dancing was to take place. His huge double-bass encased in leather on his back, he walked beside a river where the cool waters flowed along, if not sublimely, then at least with a certain lyricism.

"Why not take a dip?" he thought.

And without much further thinking he stripped and launched his body into the cool stream.

It was a magnificent evening and Smichkov's poetic nature began to be in harmony with his surroundings. But then a most sweet feeling entranced his spirits; for, having swum along a hundred paces, he saw a very lovely girl sitting on the steep bank, fishing. He held his breath, struck quite still, a prey to changing emotions: childhood memories, yearning for the past, a stirring of love.

But, oh God, he thought he was able to love no longer! Since he lost faith in humanity (when his darling wife ran off with Sabarkin, the bassoon player, his friend) his heart was filled with a sense of emptiness and he had become a misanthropist.

"What kind of life is this?" he'd asked himself more than once. "What are we living for? Life is a myth, a day-dream . . . a puppet show . . ."

But now at the feet of this sleeping beauty (it was easy to see she was asleep) he suddenly felt, despite his will, a thing in his heart akin to love. He stayed a long time before her, feasting his eyes . . .

"But that's enough . . ." he thought, breathing a deep sigh. "Farewell, lovely vision! It's time now for me to go to His Highness' ball . . ."

And with yet another glance at the lovely girl he was starting to swim back when an idea flashed across his mind.

"I must leave her a thing to remember me by!" he thought. "I'll hitch something to her line. It will be a surprise from "an unknown stranger."

Smichkov swam quietly to the bank, gathered a bunch of field and water flowers, bound them with a stalk of goose foot and hitched them to the line.

The bunch sank down and with it took the pretty float.

❖ ❖ ❖

Prudence, the natural order of things and the social position of my hero require that my love story should end just here. But, alas, the fate of an author is relentless. In clear despite of him his story will not end with the bunch of flowers. Against all sober sense and natural law the poor and humble double-bass player had to play a role of great importance in the life of a noble, rich and lovely young lady.

❖ ❖ ❖

When he reached the bank, Smichkov was horrified: he couldn't see his clothes, someone had stolen them! While he'd been gazing lovingly upon the lovely girl, some unknown villains had made off with everything, except his double-bass and his top hat.

"Curses on you, breed of snakes!" he shouted. "It's not only the loss of clothes that makes my blood boil (for clothes wear out) but the thought that I must go stark naked and offend the laws of decency."

He sat down on his double-bass case and tried to seek a way out of his terrible dilemma.

"I can't walk naked to Prince Bibulov's!" he thought. "There'll be ladies! And what's more the thieves stole my rosin when they made off with my trousers."

He thought and thought in anguish till his temples hurt.

"Ah!" At last he remembered. "Not far from the bank in the bushes there's a footbridge. Till darkness comes I can sit under that bridge and then in the dusk of evening I'll sneak to the nearest peasant's hut."

Having thought the matter over, Smichkov put on his top hat, heaved up his double-bass behind him and trudged towards the bushes. Naked, his instrument on his back, he was like some mythical demigod of the ancient world.

❖ ❖ ❖

And there, my reader, while my hero sits under the bridge and gives in to grief, we'll leave him for a while and return to the girl who was fishing. What happened to her? When she woke up and could not see her float on the water, she hurriedly tugged at the line. It tautened but neither float nor hook came up. Apparently Smichkov's bunch of flowers had become sodden and heavy in the water.

"Either a big fish is biting," she thought, "or else the hook is caught."

She tugged away at the line for a while and decided that the hook was caught.

"What a pity!" she thought. "In the evening when the fish bite so well! What shall I do?"

And without much thought the eccentric girl threw off her flimsy garments and submerged her lovely body to the marble shoulders in the stream. It wasn't easy to free the hook from the entangling bunch of flowers but work and patience won the day. After some fifteen minutes the lovely girl came radiant and happy out of the water, clutching the hook.

But an evil fate awaited her. The rogues who had stolen
Smichkov's clothes, had snatched hers too, leaving only a jar
of worms.

"Whatever shall I do now?" She burst into tears. "Can I
possibly go about looking like this? No, never! I'd rather die!
I'll wait till dusk, then go in the dark to my old nanny Agatha's
and send her home for clothes. And in the meantime I'll go
and hide under the footbridge."

My heroine, choosing the deepest grass and bending low,
ran to the bridge. Creeping under it, she saw a naked man with
musician's curls and hairy chest, screamed and lost her senses.

Smichkov was frightened too. At first he took her for a water
nymph.

"Is this a mermaid come to lure me?" he wondered and the
idea appealed for he had always had a high opinion of his looks.
"If she's not a mermaid but a human being, then how do you
explain that strange appearance? Why is she here under the
bridge? And what's the matter with her?"

While he was considering these questions, the lovely girl
came round.

"Don't kill me!" she murmured. "I'm Princess Bibulova. I
implore you! You'll get a big reward! Just now I was untangling
my hook in the water and some thieves stole away my new
dress, my boots and everything!"

"Madam," said Smichkov in a pleading voice, "they stole
my clothes as well. What's more they even took away the
rosin that was in my trousers."

Double-bass players and trombonists are usually at a loss in
crises: but Smichkov was a pleasant exception.

"Madam," he said after a little pause, "I see that my appearance embarrasses you. But you'll agree I can't go off in this
state, any more than you can. Here's what I suggest: would
you like to lie down in my double-bass case and cover yourself
with the lid? That will hide you from me . . ."

With these words Smichkov heaved his double-bass out of
the case. For a moment it seemed a profanation of his sublime

art to give up his case but his hesitation was short. The lovely girl lay down inside the case and curled up and Smichkov fastened the straps, feeling delighted that nature had given him such intelligence.

"Now, Madam, you cannot see me," he said. "Lie there and be at ease. When darkness comes, I'll carry you to your father's house. And then I can come back here for my double-bass."

When it was dusk Smichkov hoisted the case with the lovely girl on his shoulder and set off for Bibulov's *dacha*. His plan was this: he would go first to the nearest cottage, get some clothes there and then go on . . .

"Every cloud has a silver lining . . ." he reflected, stirring up the dust with his bare feet and bending under his load. "For the warm sympathy I've shown his daughter in her plight, Bibulov is sure to reward me handsomely."

"Are you quite comfortable, Madam?" he asked in the tone of a *cavalier galant* requesting her to dance a quadrille. "I beg you, do not stand on ceremony and make yourself quite at home in my case!"

Suddenly it seemed to the gallant Smichkov that before him, shrouded in darkness, two human shapes were moving. Peering more closely, he was sure it wasn't an optical illusion: the shapes were certainly moving and what's more were carrying some sort of bundles . . .

"Isn't that the thieves?" flashed into his mind. "They're carrying something. It's probably our clothes!"

Smichkov lowered his double-bass beside the path and dashed after the figures.

"Stop!" he shouted. "Stop! Seize them!"

The shapes looked round and seeing they were pursued took to their heels. The Princess heard running footsteps for a time and cries of "Stop!" Then all was still.

Smichkov kept up the chase, and very probably the lovely girl would have lain a long time in a field by the path but for a happy chance. It turned out that two of Smichkov's colleagues, Zhuchkov, the flutist, and Razmahaikin, the clarinetist, were passing at that time along that way to Bibulov's *dacha*. Stumbling upon the case, they stared at each other in surprise and flung up their arms.

"A double-bass!" said Zhuchkov. "But that's our Smichkov's double-bass. But how did it get here?"

"Something has probably happened to Smichkov," Razmahaikin decided. "Either he's drunk or he's been robbed. We'll take it with us."

Zhuchkov hoisted the case on his back and the musicians went on their way.

"What a devil of a weight!" the flutist kept grumbling all the way. "I wouldn't play this lumbering thing for anything in the world! Oh!"

Once they reached Prince Bibulov's *dacha* they put the case in the place reserved for the orchestra and went off to the buffet.

The chandeliers were just being lit. The fiancé Lakeitch, a counsellor at court and an official in the Highways Department, a very pleasant, handsome fellow, was standing in the middle of the ballroom, hands in pockets, chatting about music to Count Shkalikov.

"You know, Count," he said, "I came across a string player in Naples who worked perfect wonders. You don't believe me? On a double-bass, a common or garden double-bass, he produced such devilish trills it made you shiver. He played Strauss waltzes."

"Surely it's impossible . . ." said the Count with doubt in his voice.

"But I assure you. He even performed a Rhapsody of Liszt. I used to share a room with him and once, to pass the time, I learned from him how to play a Liszt Rhapsody on the double-bass."

"A Liszt Rhapsody . . . Hmmmm! You're joking . . ."

"You don't believe me?" laughed Lakeitch. "Very well, I'll prove it to you. Let's go over to the orchestra."

The fiancé and the count went over to the orchestra, found

the double-bass, started hurriedly to undo the straps . . . and oh, horror!

And now, as the reader, giving full rein to imagination, pictures the outcome of this musical controversy, let us return to Smichkov . . . The poor musician, not having caught the thieves, returned to the spot where he put down his case but did not see his precious burden. Bewildered, he wandered back and forth along the path a few times and, still not finding it, decided he had come to the wrong path . . .

"It's terrible!" he thought, plucking his hair and going freezing cold. "She'll suffocate in that case. I'm a murderer."

Till midnight he paced up and down the path, searching for his case, but in the end, exhausted, he set off for the footbridge.

"I'll search again at dawn," he decided.

But searching in the dawn brought just the same result and Smichkov decided to wait for nightfall under the bridge.

"I'll find her!" he muttered, taking off his top hat and clutching his hair. "Even if I search a year, I'll find her."

❖ ❖ ❖

And still today the peasants living in the place relate that in the night time a sort of naked man is to be seen, overgrown with hair and in a top hat. From under the bridge sometimes you can hear the wheezing of a double-bass.

1886

A LITTLE CRIME

❖ ❖ ❖

On his way back from his evening stroll Miguev, a collegiate assessor, stopped by a telegraph pole and sighed deeply. At that very spot, a week ago, in the evening as he was coming home from his stroll, Agnia, who used to be his house-maid, came up after him and snapped maliciously:

"Just you wait! I'll cook your goose so you'll know what it means to ruin innocent girls. I'll leave the baby on your doorstep, I'll go to court, and I'll tell your wife . . ."

And she wanted him to put five thousand roubles in the bank in her name. Miguev sighed as he remembered and once again regretted bitterly the passion of a moment that had brought him such worry and pain.

Reaching his *dacha*, he sat on the step for a breather. It was just ten o'clock with a sliver of moon peeping from behind the clouds and not a soul to be seen in the street or about the *dachas*. The old people who came there for the summer were already off to bed and the young ones were walking in the woods.

Feeling in both pockets for a match for his cigarette, Miguev brought his elbow against something soft and, as he glanced unthinkingly down under his right elbow, his face contorted with as much horror as if he'd seen a snake there beside him.

Just up against the door lay a bundle, an oblong-shaped thing tucked up in what felt like a padded quilt. One end of the bundle was slightly open and the collegiate assessor, slipping his hand into it, felt something damp and warm. Horrified, he jumped up and looked about him like a criminal seeking a way to run from his guards.

"She's gone and left it!" he hissed angrily through his teeth and clenched his fists. "There it is . . . there's . . . my . . . my little crime! Oh God!"

He went cold with fear, anger and shame. Now what was he to do? What would his wife say if she found out? What would his colleagues say? His Excellency, of course, would dig him in the ribs, chuckle and say: "Congratulations! Ha-ha-ha! . . . Grey hair in your beard but the devil's down below! You rascal, Semeon Erastovitch!" All the neighbours would know his secret now and respectable mothers of families, very probably, would turn him from their doors. They reported such things in the papers and so the humble name of Miguev would go all over Russia . . .

The middle window of the *dacha* was open and he clearly heard his wife, Anna Filipovna, laying the table for supper; in the yard, just inside the gate, Yermolai, the watchman, was mournfully strumming his balalaika. Let the baby only wake up and squeal and his secret was known. Miguev felt an overpowering desire to do something quickly.

"Get a move on," he muttered, "a move on! This minute while no-one's looking. I'll take it somewhere, set it down on someone else's porch . . ."

Miguev picked up the bundle in one hand and quietly, with steady step lest he arouse suspicion, went down the street.

"What an astonishing mess to be in!" he thought, trying to assume a look of unconcern. "A collegiate assessor going down the street with a baby! Oh God, if anyone sees and realises what it's all about, I'm sunk.

"I'll put it on this doorstep . . . No, wait, the window's open, someone might be looking out. Where shall I put it? Ah, I know what, I'll take it to the *dacha* of Melkin, the merchant. Merchants are rich people and good-hearted; they might say thank you and adopt it.

And Miguev decided to take the child at once to Melkin's although the merchant's *dacha* was on the last street of all, by the river side.

"If only he doesn't start screaming or wriggling out of the bundle!" thought the collegiate assessor. "Well, here we are: thank you very much, what a surprise! I'm carrying a human being under my arm like a briefcase. A human being with a soul and feelings like all the rest of us. If he's lucky and the Melkins adopt him, he may very likely turn out to be somebody. Very likely turn out to be a professor of some sort, a general, a writer. Anything's possible in this world! Now I'm carrying him under my arm like some old rubbish, but in thirty years or forty, very likely, I'll have to stand to attention when I see him . . ."

As Miguev went by a long row of fences along a narrow alley deserted under thick shadows of lime trees, it suddenly seemed to him he was doing something cruel and wrong.

"That's what it is, when you look at it, mean! So mean you can't think of anything meaner. Why am I carting this unhappy child from door to door? Is it his fault he's been born? What harm has he done me? We're all scoundrels! We like to go on the spree but the innocent babies have to foot the bill. It's sickening to think of all this mess. I've been dissolute and now this child has a grim fate in store. If I leave him at the Melkins', they'll put him in an orphanage, among strangers all the time, always tied by regulations . . . no love, no affection, no cuddling . . . They'll apprentice him then to a shoemaker. He'll take to drink and foul language, pine with hunger . . . A shoemaker, but the son of a collegiate assessor, of good family. My flesh and blood! . . ."

Miguev came from the shadows of the lime trees to the bright moonlight of the road, unwrapped the bundle and looked at the baby.

"Asleep!" he murmured. "Well, how do you like that, the rascal has a hooked nose like his father? Asleep with no inkling that his father's looking at him . . . It's a drama, old friend . . . well, forgive me . . . Please forgive me, old friend . . . Seems you were born to this . . ."

The collegiate assessor blinked and felt a kind of shiver over his cheeks . . . He wrapped up the baby, put him under his arm and strode forward. All along the way, right up to the Melkins' *dacha*, moral questions worried his head and conscience plagued him.

"If I were a decent and honourable man," he thought, "I wouldn't give a damn. I'd take this little lad to Anna Filipovna, kneel to her and say: 'Forgive me, I'm a sinner. Tear me to shreds but we won't ruin this innocent child. We've no children, let's adopt him.' She's a good sort, she'd agree. And then I'd have my child with me . . . Eh!"

He reached the Melkins' *dacha* and hesitated . . .

He imagined himself sitting in the parlour at home, reading the paper while a little boy with a hooked nose played with the tassel of his dressing gown; but at the same time he pictured his colleagues winking and His Excellency digging him in the ribs and chuckling . . . As well as qualms of conscience he felt a kind of tenderness, affection and sadness . . .

The collegiate assessor carefully laid the child on the porch step and flapped his hand . . . Again he felt a kind of shiver across his face.

"Forgive me, old friend. I'm a scoundrel!" he muttered. "Don't think badly of me!"

He stepped a pace back but immediately gave a determined grunt and said:

"Oh, come what may, I don't give a damn! I'm taking him, let people say what they like!"

Miguev picked up the baby and hurried back.

"Let them say what they like," he thought. "I'll go in right away, kneel down and say: 'Anna Filipovna.' She's a good sort, she'll understand . . . And we'll bring him up. If it's a boy, we'll call him Vladimir, Anna, if it's a girl. A comfort for us he or she will be in our old age . . ."

And he did just as he'd decided. Weeping, near to fainting with shame and fear, full of hope and a diffuse delight, he went into the *dacha* to his wife and fell on his knees before her . . .

"Anna Filipovna," he said, sobbing and laying the baby on the floor. "Don't condemn me before you hear me. I'm a sinner. This is my child . . . You remember Agnia, to be sure . . . The devil tempted me to it . . ."

And beside himself with fear and shame he didn't wait for a reply but jumped to his feet and ran like a beaten dog into the open air.

"I'll stay out in the yard till she calls me," he thought, "give her time to come to her senses and think it over . . ."

Yermolai, the watchman, went by with his balalaika, glanced at him and shrugged his shoulders. A minute later he came by again and again he shrugged.

"Here's a funny how-do-you-do!" he muttered, grinning. "And no mistake! Aksinia, the washerwoman, was here just now, Semeon Erastovitch. Like a fool she put her baby on the steps here and came in with me for a bit . . . and somebody's been up and off with it . . . Fancy that!"

"What? What's that you say?" shouted Miguev at the top of his voice.

Yermolai, attributing his master's anger to a different cause, scratched his head and sighed.

"Sorry, Semeon Erastovitch," he said, "but it's the summer holiday time . . . and you can't get by without it . . . without a woman, I mean . . ."

And seeing his master's eyes staring with such bitter astonishment, he cleared his throat guiltily and went on:

"It's a sin, of course, but what can you do? You won't let us have strange women in the house, that's a fact, but where are we to get any of our own? . . . Before, when little Agnia was living here, I didn't have any strange women in, because there was one here for me . . . but nowadays, well, you can see yourself, sir . . . you can't manage without a woman . . . But when little Agnia was here, there was no breaking rules because . . ."

"Get out, you scoundrel!" shouted Miguev, stamped his feet and went back into the room.

Anna Filipovna, astonished and angry, was sitting in the same place, on the edge of tears, not taking her eyes off the baby.

"Now, now . . ." muttered Miguev, pale, twisting his mouth into a smile. "I was joking . . . It's not mine . . . but the washerwoman's . . . I was joking . . . Take it to the watchman."

1887

FROM SIBERIA

❖ ❖ ❖

I

"Why do you have it so cold in Siberia?"

"It's as God wills!" replies my coachman.

Yes, it is May already, in Russia the forests are green and nightingales are singing, and in the south acacia and lilac have long been in bloom; but here, on the road from Tyumen to Tomsk, the earth is brown, the forests bare, dull ice lies over the lakes and there is snow still on the shores and in gullies.

For all that, I have never in my life seen so much wild-fowl. I watch wild duck move over fields, swim in pools and wayside ditches, plough up the earth almost by my carriage and fly up lazily into the birch forest. Into the silence comes suddenly a melodious sound, you look up and see, not far above, a pair of cranes, and for some reason you feel sad. Wild duck are flying by and a line of splendid swans, as white as snow, pass overhead. Sandpipers sigh everywhere and seagulls complain . . .

We overtake two covered wagons and a crowd of peasants and their women. They are migrants.

"Which region are you from?"

"From Kursk."

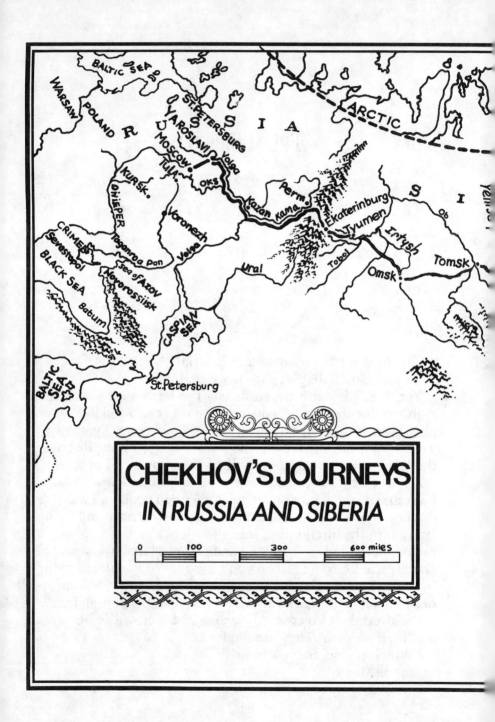

CHEKHOV'S JOURNEYS
IN RUSSIA AND SIBERIA

0   100   300   600 miles

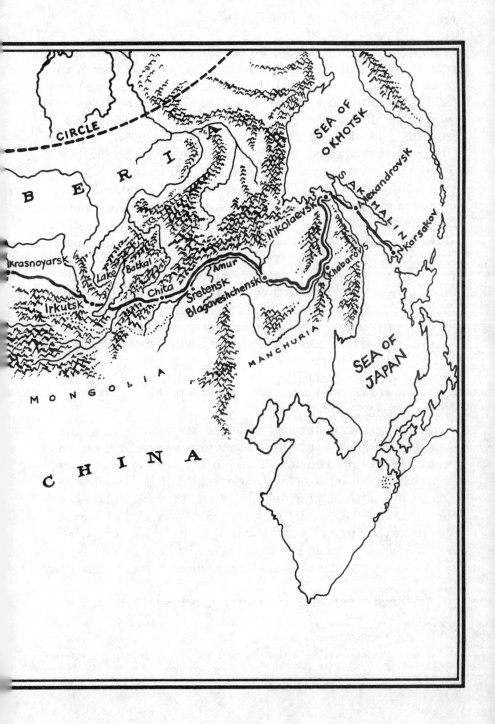

Behind the others a man, unlike them, trudges along. His chin is clean-shaven, he has grey moustaches, and there's an unusual fold at the back of his kaftan. Under his arms are two fiddles, wrapped in a shawl. Pointless to ask who he is or where the fiddles comes from. He's feckless, unstable, sick, feels the cold and is partial to vodka, a timid man who all his life has been unwanted, first by his father, then by his brother. They neither set him up, nor found a wife for him. What a poor fellow he is! He shivered over his work, got drunk on a couple of glasses, chattered a lot of nonsense, and only knew how to play the fiddle and romp with the children on the stove. He played in taverns and at weddings and in the open country, oh yes, how he played! But then his brother sold their cottage, cattle and all, and set off with his family for distant Siberia. And this lonely fellow has come too—nowhere else to go. And brought with him both his fiddles . . . And now he's here, he will freeze in Siberian cold, wilt quietly and die, in silence, so that no one notices, and his fiddles, stuck in a local village to rejoice or grieve there, will end up with some alien twopenny clerk or an exile; the clerk's children will tear the strings, break the bridge and pour water into the soundbox . . . Go back home, old fellow!

I saw migrants before as I travelled by steamer along the Kama: I remember a peasant of about forty with a light brown beard. He sat on a bench on deck, at his feet his bundles of household goods on which his ragged children lay huddled up against the harsh wind which blows over the barren shores of the Kama. His face said: "I am resigned to this." In his eyes was irony, but irony directed within, at his own soul, at all his past life which had so cruelly deceived him.

"It won't get worse!" he said and smiled with only his top lip.

I remained silent, asked no questions but a minute later he repeated:

"It won't get worse!"

"It will get worse!"—said a red-headed, sharp-featured peasant with a fixed stare from the next bench—"It will get worse!"

The people now trudging along beside their covered wagons are silent. Their faces are serious, intent . . . I look at them and think: to break forever from a life which no longer seems normal, to sacrifice for that your native place and people, only a remarkable man can do it, a hero . . .

A little later, we reach a staging post for convicts. Thirty or forty of them come along the road, fetters clanking, soldiers with rifles on either side, and behind them—two carts. One convict looks like an Armenian priest, another, tall, with eagle nose and great forehead, I seem to have seen somewhere behind the counter of a chemist's shop, and a third has a pale, weary and serious face like that of a fasting monk. You haven't time to look at them all. The convicts and soldiers are worn out: the road is bad, they haven't the strength to go on . . . To the village where they will spend the night, it's another seven miles. And when they get there, after a quick bite, washed down by brick-red tea, they'll tumble down to sleep, and bugs will swarm over them—the bitterest enemies, undefeatable, of a man desperate to sleep.

In the evening the earth starts to freeze and mud turns into hummocks. The carriage jumps, squeaks and creaks in different tones. It is cold. No dwellings, no people. Nothing stirs in dark air, there are no sounds but the jolting of the carriage on the frozen earth, and when you light a cigarette, two or three ducks fly up noisily from beside the road, awakened by the glow . . .

We reach a river. We will have to cross by ferry. On the bank there's not a soul.

"They've gone across, damn their hides!" says my coachman. "We'll have to roar, sir."

To cry out in pain, weep, call for help, make any kind of cry, that, here, is roaring. In Siberia not only bears roar, but sparrows and mice. "A cat got her and she roared"—they say of a mouse.

We start to roar. The river is broad and the other bank is out
of sight in dark . . . In the river damp our feet freeze, then all
our bodies . . . We roar for half an hour, an hour, but there's
no ferry. Soon it gets on my nerves, the water, the stars stud-
ding the sky, and this heavy, sepulchral silence. In boredom I
talk with the old man, and learn that he's been married sixteen
years, that he's had eighteen children, of whom only three
have died, that his mother and father are still alive; they are
dissenters, they don't smoke and in all their lives have seen
no town but Ishim, but he himself, my coachman as a young
man, fell from grace and smoked. I learn from him that in this
dark, forbidding river swim white salmon, turbot and pike,
but it's worth no one's while to catch them.

But now, at last, we hear a measured plash and something
clumsy and dark appears on the river. It's the ferry. It look like
a not very big barge; aboard are five oarsmen, and their pairs
of long oars with broad paddles are like the claws of crayfish.

As they pull in to the shore, the oarsmen start grumbling.
They grumble spitefully, without reason, clearly half asleep.
Listening to their choice swearing, you may imagine that not
only my coachman and the horses and themselves have mothers, but the water too, the ferry and the oars. Their softest and
least offensive oath is "Ulcers on you!" or "Ulcers foul your
mouth!" What sort of ulcers they wish on you here, I did not
understand, although I made inquiries. I'm wearing a sheepskin jacket, big boots and a cap: in the dark they do not see
that I am a "sir," and one oarsman croaks at me:

"Eh, you ulcer you, don't stand and gape! Unharness that
horse!"

We go aboard the ferry. The ferrymen bend to their oars.
They are not local peasants but exiles, banished by society
because of their criminal lives. In the village, where they were
sent, they are out of place—bored, unable or unaccustomed to
plough, and this alien earth is not dear to them, for they were
transported here. Their faces are haggard, dissolute, brow-
beaten. And what expressions are on those faces! It is all too
evident that they sailed here on convict barges, chained in

pairs by the wrist, tramped the highway from staging post to staging post, lodged at night in log huts, where bugs insufferably bit them and they were numb with cold to the fibres of their brain; and now, day and night in the cold water, seeing nothing but barren river-banks, the heat draining from their bodies all the time, what else have they, what is left in life, but vodka and a whore, a whore and vodka. In this world they are no longer people, only beasts, and in the next world, says my friend, the coachman, evil will be their fate: for their sins they will go to hell.

2

On the night before the 6th May, an old man of about sixty, my coachman, drives out with me from the big village of Abatskoe; before harnessing the horses, he took a steam bath and put cupping glasses on his back to draw the blood. Why? He says he has pain in the small of his back. It does not trouble him much in summer, when he's on the move and has plenty to say, but he walks badly. I think he has spinal ataxia.

I sit in a high, uncovered, springless carriage, drawn by two horses. The old man swings his whip and cries out, but his cry is not as it was, he only coos or moans like an Egyptian dove.

At the sides of the road and far off to the horizon are snaky lines of light: last year's grass is burning, they fire it at this time. It is damp and slow to kindle, so that fiery snakes creep slowly, burst out in some places, then subside, then flare again. Fires flicker with sparks and above each is a white cloud of smoke. It is beautiful when fire suddenly engulfs high grass: a fiery pillar rises two yards high over the land, thrusts a huge cloud of smoke above it into the sky, and then suddenly falls as if to vanish through the earth. It is even more beautiful when little fiery snakes twist among birch trees; the forest is lit through and through, white trunks gleam distinctly and the shadows of the trees ripple with flecks of light. Such illumination is rather frightening.

Towards us, at full speed, thundering over mounds, comes
a postal troika. My old coachman hurriedly swings to the right,
and there and then the huge and heavy postal wagon flies past
us, the driver on top. But at once another thundering noise is
heard: another troika is coming towards us, and that too at
full speed. We hasten again to swing to the right, but to my
utter astonishment, this troika for some reason turns left, not
right, and flies headlong at us. "God, what if we collide?" I've
barely time to ask the question, when a crash resounds, our
pair of horses and the troika's tangle in a dark mass, our carriage rears up, and I fall to the ground, my trunks and bundles
falling on top of me . . . And, as I lie, stunned, on the ground,
I hear yet a third troika coming. "Well, this one will kill me,
that's certain!" But, glory be to God, I have no broken bones,
no painful injuries, and I can get up. I jump to my feet, run
out of the way and shout in a voice not my own:

"Stop, stop!"

From the depths of the wagon a figure appears and grabs the
reins, and this third troika stops just as it reaches my tumbled
baggage.

Three minutes pass by in silence. In a blunt bewilderment,
as if we cannot understand what has happened. Shafts are
broken, harness torn, arching beams with hanging bells lying
on the ground, horses snorting: they are stunned too, and, it
seems, badly hurt. My old coachman, grunting and moaning,
gets up from the ground; the first two troikas come back, and
soon a fourth arrives, and a fifth . . .

Then a violent row starts.

"Ulcers on you!" shouts a coachman, pitching into us. "Ulcers foul your mouth! Where were your bloody eyes, you old
dog?"

"Well, whose fault was it?" moans my old man. "Yours,
then you start swearing at us!"

As far as I understand from the wrangling, the cause of
the collision is this. Five troikas were making for Abatskoe,
carrying mail: according to instructions the first coachman is
supposed to drive slowly, but this fellow, bored stiff and eager

to be in the warm, lashed his horses on at top speed; the coachmen in the next four troikas were asleep; so, with no one in control, their horses ran following the others at top speed. If I had been asleep in my carriage, or if the third troika had been hard on the heels of the second, I wouldn't have been so lucky.

The coachmen go on cursing at the top of their voices, loud enough to be heard seven miles away. It is unbearable. How much wit, malice and mental filth is spent in inventing dirty words and phrases to insult and defile a man in all he holds sacred, dear and fine. Only Siberian coachmen and ferrymen know how to swear like this, and they picked it up, they say, from convicts. And the loudest and nastiest of the swearers is the man who caused the accident.

"Stop your swearing, idiot!" shouts my old coachman.

"What's that?" shouts the guilty one, a lad of about nineteen, thrusting his face threateningly into his. "What's that?"

"You heard!"

"What? Answer me: what are you saying? I'll take a lump of shaft and bash you with it, you ulcer!"

It seems they'll come to blows. In the night, before dawn, within this savage cursing mob, fires burning near and far, consuming the grass, but failing at all to warm the night air, restive horses nearby, clustered together and neighing, I feel a loneliness hard to describe.

My old friend moves off, lifting his legs stiffly—in pain, I think—goes around the coaches and horses, unties ropes and belts where he can, and binds the broken shaft with them; then, lighting match after match, he creeps along the road on all fours, looking for the traces. My own baggage belt comes in handy. Now in the east dawn is breaking, and for a time awakened wild geese have been squawking. At last the coachmen drive away, and we stand on the road and do repairs. We try to travel further but the bound shaft goes—crack—and we have to stop again ... It is cold.

Somehow or other we drag along to a village. We stop near a two-storied log cabin.

"Ilya Ivanich, anyone at home?" shouts my old friend.

"Yes," comes a gruff voice from a window.

Inside the cabin a tall man in a red shirt comes towards me, barefoot, half-asleep and dreamily smiling.

"We're beating the bed-bugs, friend," he says, scratching and smiling more broadly. "It's on purpose we don't heat the room. In the cold the bugs don't walk."

Here bugs and cockroaches do not crawl, they walk; travellers do not travel, they run. "Where are you running to, sir?" they ask, meaning, "Where are you going?"

While they grease the carriage and set the bells ringing, and while Ilya Ivanich, who will be my next driver, is getting dressed, I find a comfortable little place in a corner, lay my head on a sack of something, probably grain, and at once heavy sleep overpowers me; I dream of my bed and my room, dream that I'm sitting at my desk at home and telling my people that my two horses collided with a postal troika; but two or three minutes pass and I sense Ilya Ivanich taking my hand and hear him say:

"Get up, friend! The horses are ready!"

What humilation I feel for my sluggishness and loathing of the cold, which runs like a snake over my back, along and across! We're on the go again . . . It is already light, the sky becoming golden before the sun comes up. The road, the grass in the fields and the pitiful young birch trees are covered with rime, as if crystallized. Somewhere heath-cocks are thrashing about . . .

8th May

3

On the Siberian Highway, from Tyumen to Tomsk, are neither settlements nor farming estates, only some big villages, some fifteen, twenty or even thirty miles apart. You find no estates for there are no landowners; you see neither factories nor mills nor coaching inns . . . The only things to remind you of man are telegraph wires, whining in the wind, and milestones.

In every village is a church, and sometimes there are two; and it seems there are schools in all the villages. The large log cabins are often of two stories with plank roofs. Near each cabin on a fence or a birch tree stands a starling's house, so low that you can reach it with your hand. Everyone loves starlings here, even the cats don't touch them. There are no gardens.

At five o'clock in the morning, after an icy night and an exhausting ride, I am sitting in the log cabin of an independent coachman, in his sitting room and drinking tea. The room is bright and spacious and has furnishing of which our peasants in Kursk or Moscow can only dream. Surprisingly clean too: no dust, no stains. The walls are white, the floor all of wood, dyed, or covered with coloured carpets; there are two tables, a sofa, a cupboard with crockery, and at the windows stand flower-pots. In the corner is a bed, on it a huge mountain of feathers and pillows in red pillow-cases; to clamber up this mountain you have to use a chair, then slide into it and sink. Siberians love to sleep on softness.

Around an ikon in a corner are spread out on both sides some popular prints; the Czar in several portraits, Georgi the Victorious, "European Monarchs" with the Shah of Persia for some reason among them, portraits of saints with Latin and German inscriptions, the faces and shoulders of Battenberg and Skobelev, then more saints . . . The walls are decorated with sweet-papers and vodka and cigarette labels, cheap things quite out of place beside the solid bed and the dyed and carpeted floor. But what are people to do? Demand for artistry is great here, but God has sent no artists. Look at the door, with a tree painted on it that has blue and red flowers and some birds that look more like fish; this tree is growing out of a vase, a vase that a European must have painted, in fact, an exile; he has painted a circle on the ceiling too and a pattern on the stove. Simple painting but more than local people can do. For nine months the artist never took off his gloves or unbent his fingers; forty degrees of frost, then the meadows flooded for fifteen miles or so, and then a brief summer—the back aches with labour and the sinews swell. So when can he paint? All year round he fights a cruel battle with nature, and is neither painter, musician, nor singer. In this landscape you rarely hear a concertina; nor do you expect a coachman to burst into song.

A door is open and across a passage I see another room, bright and with a wooden floor. Busy work is going on. The lady of the house, a woman of about twenty-five, tall, slender, with a kind and gentle face, is kneading dough at a table; the morning sun shines on her eyes, her breast, her arms, and it is as if she is imbuing the dough with sunlight; her younger sister is frying pancakes, a cook is pouring boiling water over a piglet whose throat has just been cut, and the man of the house is making felt boots. Only the old people are doing nothing. Grandmother is sitting on the stove, legs dangling, sighing and moaning; grandfather is lying on a board bed and coughing, but, noticing me, he climbs down and comes across the passage to the room where I am. He is eager to talk ... He starts by saying that spring is colder this year than for a very long time. Imagine, tomorrow is St. Nicholas' Day and the day after will be Ascension Day, and still there is snow in the night, and a woman froze to death on the road to the village; cattle are wasting away from hunger and calves have bloody flux from the frost ... Then he asks me where I come from, where I'm running to, whether I'm married, and whether old women are right to say there'll be a war.

I hear a weeping child. And now I notice that between the bed and stove there hangs a little cradle. The lady of the house flings down her dough and rushes across into this room.

"Something happened to us, sir," she tells me, as she rocks the cradle and gives a gentle smile. "Two months ago a woman came to us with a little child. Of the middle class ... Like a fine lady by her dress ... She had given birth in Tykaninsk, and christened the baby there; after the birth she was in no condition to journey, and she began to live in our house, here in this room. She said she was married but who knows? It wasn't written on her face, and she had no passport with her. Perhaps the child is illegitimate . . ."

"It's not for us to judge her," mutters grandfather.

"She lived with us a week," she goes on, "then told us: 'I'm going to Omsk to my husband, and will have to leave my Sasha with you. I'll come to fetch him in a week or so. I fear that now he'd freeze to death on the road.' I said to her: 'Please listen, my lady. God sends children into the world. To some couples he gives ten children, to some twelve; but on me and my husband he has not even bestowed a single one. Leave your Sasha with us and we will treat him like our own little son.' She thought it over and said 'Please wait. I'll ask my husband and in a week's time I'll send you a letter. I daren't do it without his permission.' She left Sasha with us and went away. And now two months have gone by, and she has neither come nor sent a letter. It's a punishment from God. We've fallen in love with Sasha, like our own, but we don't know whether he is ours or another's."

"You must send a letter to the lady," I advise her.

"We should. It stands to reason!" says her husband from the passage.

He comes into the room and looks at me in silence: won't I give him further advice?

"But how can we write to her?" says his wife. "She didn't tell us her family name. She was just Maria Petrovna. And Omsk is a big town, isn't it, we can't find her there. As well seek the wind in the field."

"Yes, it stands to reason. We won't be able to find her," agrees her husband, and looks at me as if to say: "Help me, for God's sake!"

"We're used to Sasha now," she says, giving the baby a dummy. "When he starts to cry, day or night, it touches the heart, and it's as if all our home is changed. But an unlucky day will dawn, and she'll come and take him from us."

Anton Chekhov

Her eyes redden and fill with tears, and she rushes out. Her husband nods after her, smiles wryly and says:

"She's become used to him . . . That's evident. It's a pity."

But he himself has become used to the child, it's a pity for him too, but he's a man and it would embarrass him to admit it.

What fine people they are! As I drink tea and hear about Sasha, my things are in the carriage out there in the courtyard. To my question, won't they be stolen, they answer with a smile:

"Who steals here? Here they don't sneak off with things by night."

And indeed, all the way along the road, I have not heard of people stealing from travellers. Morals in this respect are splendid, there's a fine tradition. I'm quite convinced that, if I drop some money in the carriage, the independent coachman who finds it will return it, he won't even look in my wallet. I have travelled little with coachmen from posting stations, but I can say this: in the complaint books I read there out of boredom, I saw only one complaint of theft: a traveller lost a bag containing boots, but due to the diligence of the manager there were no grave consequences, for the bag was soon found and returned to the traveller. It's unpleasant even to talk of theft on the highway. You don't hear about it. And as for the wandering tramps, with whom they so frightened me in talk, why, here they seem about as frightening as hares or ducks.

With tea they give me pancakes from wheat flour, with curds and eggs, and pastry loaves. The pancakes are thin and greasy but the loaves are tasty. They remind me of those yellow porous bagels they sell in the bazaars in Taganrog and Rostov-On-Don. Everywhere on the Siberian Highway bread is deliciously baked. They bake bread every day and in large quantities. Wheat flour is cheap here: thirty to forty copeks a pood.

But bread alone is not enough to satisfy. If at midday you ask for something cooked, you are only offered "duck soup" and nothing else. And it's uneatable: a turbid liquid with little lumps of duck and giblets swimming in it, nasty and sickening to look at. In every dwelling there is game. In Siberia there are no game laws and they shoot birds all the year round. But they are not in the least likely to eliminate the wild fowl. In the thousand miles or so from Tyumen to Tomsk there are many wild fowl, but you don't find a single decent rifle, and only one in a hundred marksmen knows how to shoot birds in flight. Usually a marksman crawls on his belly through wet grass and fires out of bushes at a sitting bird from a distance of twenty to thirty paces; his clumsy rifle misfires five times over, and when it does fire, kicks back hard against his shoulder or cheek. If he manages to hit the target, it causes him no little trouble; he takes off his boots and trousers and wades into the cold water. Here there are no hunting dogs.

9th May

4

A cold and bitter wind is blowing and the rains have begun, pouring unceasingly day and night. At a point some thirteen miles from the Irtysh, the peasant Fedor Pavlovich, to whom my independent coachman has brought me, tells me it is impossible to travel further, as the meadows between here and the river have been flooded by the rains; yesterday Kuzma came from Pustinskoe, and he and his horses nearly drowned; we will have to wait.

"But for how long?" I ask.

"Who knows? Ask God."

I go into a log cabin. An old man in a red shirt is sitting in a room there, breathing heavily and coughing. I give him Doverov powder. It relieves him, but he doesn't believe in medicine, and says he got better because he "sat it out."

I sit and think things over: should I stay the night here? But the old man will cough all the time, and there are sure to be bed-bugs, and who can say whether tomorrow the floods won't have spread further? No, it's better to go on.

"Fedor Pavlovich," I call, "let's start out. I'm not going to wait."

"Just as you like!" is his curt reply. "As long as we're not in the water all night."

We set off. It isn't raining, and, as they say, we rattle on with all our might; my carriage is open to the sky. For five miles we travel at a canter along the muddy road.

"Well, the weather's holding!" says Fedor Pavlovich. "I haven't been this way for a while, I admit, but I don't see the floods that scared Kuzma. Perhaps God will be good to us and we'll get through."

But then before our eyes there spreads an enormous lake. These are the flooded meadows. Wind is blowing freely over them, howling, stirring up surges. But here and there are little islands, and as yet unflooded strips of land. Bridges and pontoons mark the highway, awash and sodden and nearly all loose from their moorings. Beyond the lake stretches the high bank of the Irtysh, brown and sullen, and over it hang heavy grey clouds; at places along the bank falling snow glimmers white.

We begin to drive over the lake. It isn't deep, our wheels are only about six inches under water. The going would be tolerable if it weren't for the bridges, but at each of these we have to climb out and stand in the muddy water. Before the carriage can mount the bridge, we have to collect boards and logs that are scattered about and shove them under loose parts of it. Then the horses are led over one by one. Fedor Pavlovich unharnesses the outer two and gives them me to look after. I hold them by their cold and muddy bridle reins, and they are restive and pull back, the wind tries to rip my clothing from me, and rain beats painfully into my face. Shall we turn back? Fedor Pavlovich is silent, clearly waiting for me to decide; but I stay silent too.

We take one bridge by assault, a second and a third ... In one place we are bogged down in mud, in another the horses are obstinate and ducks and seagulls fly over and seem to mock us. From the face of Fedor Pavlovich, his unhurried movements and silence, I see that it is not the first time he has struggled in this way, that he has known worse, and has been accustomed for a long time to muddy quagmires, water and cold rain. He has such life in him!

We reach a little island. There is a small cabin without a roof: two horses tread wet manure. At a call from Fedor Pavlovich a bearded peasant comes out, carrying a long stick and proceeds to take us along our way. He leads us in silence, measuring the depth of water with his stick and testing for firmness. He guides us to a long narrow strip which he calls "a backbone." We are to follow this backbone, and, when it ends, turn left, then right, and come to another backbone, which goes all the way to the ferry.

The air darkens. There are no more ducks nor seagulls. The peasant has shown us the way and turned back. The first backbone comes to an end and we are in the water again. We move left, then right, and reach the other backbone, which stretches as far as the river.

The Irtysh is broad. If a swimmer tried to cross in time of flood, he would sink without trace. The opposite bank is high, steep and quite barren. There is a hollow depression in it, and Fedor Pavlovich says that the highway goes uphill there to Pustinkoe, the village we are making for. The bank at this side drops to the water from a height of about two feet: it is bare, crumbly and honeycombed. Turgid, white-crested waves lap sullenly there, then suddenly draw back as if repelled by this sullen crumbling bank, where it seems nothing can live but toads and the wraiths of great sinners. The Irtysh does not howl or roar but sepulchral sounds murmur below. A cursed place it seems!

We reach the log cabin where the ferrymen live. One comes out and says we can't go across because of the bad weather. We will have to wait until morning.

I spend the night there. I hear the snores of the ferrymen and my coachman, rain beating on the windows and wind moaning, and the deep sepulchral murmuring of the Irtysh . . . In the early morning I go to the river. It is raining still, but the wind has quietened, yet all the same it's impossible to cross by ferry. They take me across on a boat.

A company of independent peasants operates the crossing here; there is not a single exile among them, they are all local men. Decent, good-natured people. When I have crossed the river and climb a slippery hill towards the road where a horse is waiting, they call after me, wishing me a happy journey, good health and success in what I'm doing . . . But the Irtysh still murmurs sullenly . . .

12th May

5

Curse these floods! In Kolivan they will not give me post horses. They say the fields are flooded as far as the Ob, it's impossible to go on. They are holding back till further notice.

A clerk at the posting stage advises me to make my own way as far as a place called Viun, and from there to Krasni Yar; from Krasni Yar I can go about eight miles by boat to Dubrovino, and there I can get post horses. I take his advice, go first to Viun, then to Krasni Yar . . . There they direct me to a certain Andrei who has a boat.

"Yes, I've a boat right enough!" says Andrei, a lean, brown-bearded man of about fifty, "I have a boat. Early this morning it took the district clerk to Dubrovino and will soon be back. While you're waiting, have some tea."

I drink the tea, then climb the mountain of feather bed and pillows . . . I awake and ask about the boat. It's not back yet. In the room, to make it warm for me, some peasant women light the stove and then bake some bread. The room warms up, the bread is baked, but still there's no boat.

"They sent a useless fellow!" sighs Andrei, shaking his head. "Clumsy as a woman he is, the wind must have frightened him and he's not coming. What can you do? Would you like some more tea, sir? You must be fed up."

A sort of idiot, in a battered smock and barefoot, soaked to the skin, drags wood and a bucket of water into the passage. As he does so, he peers across at me. He thrusts out his tousled, unkempt head, mutters something, moos like a calf—and is gone. Looking at his wet face and staring eyes and hearing his voice, you feel that soon you'll be delirious yourself.

In the afternoon a very big and very fat man comes to see Andrei. He has a broad bull-like head and huge fists like a plump Russian innkeeper. His name is Piotr Petrovich. He lives in the next village where he and his brother own fifty horses. He provides transport for local people and troikas for the posting stage, ploughs the land, trades in cattle, and now he is on his way to Kolivan to negotiate some business.

"You from Russia?" he asks me.

"Yes, from Russia."

"You're not the only one. Someone came to us in Tomsk. He turned up his nose, as if he'd travelled all the world. And now it's in the papers that they're bringing a railway here. Tell me, sir, what will it be like? It works by steam, I know that. But if, say, it has to go through a village, won't it smash the wooden houses and crush the people?

I explain to him, and he listens attentively and says:

"How do you like that?"

From our talk I learn that he's been in Tomsk and Irkutsk and Irbit, and that, when he was already married, he taught himself to read and write. He looks down on Andrei who has only been to Tomsk and listens to him without interest. If he is offered or given something, he says politely: "Don't trouble yourself."

Andrei and his guest sit down to have tea. A young girl, the wife of Andrei's son, brings the tea on a tray and makes a low bow. They take the cups and drink in silence. At the side of the room, by the stove, a samovar is bubbling. Once more I climb the mountain of feather bed and pillows, lie there and read; then I come down to write. Time passes, a deal of time, and the girl is still bowing to them and they are still drinking tea.

"Be-ba!"—shouts the idiot from the doorway—"Me-ma!"

Still there is no boat! It darkens in the yard, and in the room they light a tallow candle. Piotr Petrovich keeps asking me where I am going and why, whether there'll be a war, how much my revolver costs, but then he tires of talking; he sits silently at the table, props up his cheeks with his fists, and becomes sunk in thought. A midge burns in the candle. The door opens noiselessly and the idiot comes in and sits on a trunk; he bares his arms to the shoulders: they are emaciated, thin as drumsticks. He sits and stares at the candle.

"Get out!" shouts Andrei. "Get out!"

"Me-ma!" he moans, bends his back and goes into the passage. "Be-ba!"

Rain beats on the windows. Andrei and his guest sit down to duck soup. They are not hungry, eat out of boredom . . . Then the girl spreads feather beds and pillows on the floor and Andrei and his guest undress and lie down side by side.

How boring it is! To divert myself, I go in thought to my native region where already it is spring and no rain is beating on the windows, but, as if in malice, I recall a dry, grey, useless life; it seems that there too a midge burns in a candle and they're shouting "Me-ma! Be-ba!" I have no wish to return.

I spread my sheepskin jacket on the floor, lie on it and set a candle near. Piotr Petrovich lifts his head and looks at me.

"This is what I want to explain to you," he says in a low voice so that Andrei does not hear. "People here in Siberia are crude and untalented. Sheepskin jackets come here from Russia and cotton and crockery and nails, but they can't make anything themselves. They plough the land and drive people about in carriages, and that's all . . . They don't even know how to catch fish. Boring folk, God help us, so boring! You live among them and put on a lot of fat, but for your mind and soul there's nothing . . . It's a pity to look at them, for God's sake . . . A Siberian is worthy enough, his heart's in the right place; he doesn't steal or insult people; he doesn't drink all that much. A sterling fellow, you may say. But look, he'll lose himself for a brass farthing or less, quite uselessly, like a fly or a midge, say. Just ask him: for what reason do you live?"

"Man works, eats his fill, puts on his clothes"—I say—
"What else does he need?"

"For all that, he has to understand what his purpose is in
living. They must understand that in Russia."

"No, they don't."

"It's not an impossible thing," says Piotr Petrovich thought-
fully. "A man is not a horse. There is no truth among us in
Siberia. If there ever was, it's dead and gone. I'm a wealthy
man, I'm strong, I've influence in local courts. Tomorrow I
could accuse the man of the house here. Because of what I say,
he'd rot in prison, his children be cast out into the world.
There's no check on what I do, and no defence for him—
because we live without truth here . . . On our birth certifi-
cates they call us people, Piotrs and Andreis, but once let
loose, we're wolves. For all the reason that God has given us
. . . It's no joke, it's a terrible thing, but the man of the house
lay down here and only crossed himself three times, as if that's
all that's needed; he makes money and hides it, you see, he
has a hundred and eight salted away, he's buying brand new
horses, but does he ask what it's all for? Why go on taking and
taking? He asks himself, but he doesn't understand: his mind's
too small.

Piotr Petrovich goes on talking for a long time . . . And
then at last he stops; it's daylight already and the roosters are
crowing.

"Me-ma!"—moans the idiot—"Be-ba!"

And still there is no boat.

13th May

6

In Dubrovino they give me horses and I travel further. But at
a point thirty miles from Tomsk they tell me again that it's
impossible to go further, the river Tom has flooded fields and
the highway. Again I'll have to proceed by boat. And it's the
same story as at Krasni Yar: the boat has gone to the other

side, but can't return because of strong winds and high waves
. . . We will have to wait!

In the morning snow falls, covering the earth to a depth of
two and a half inches (it's the 14th of May!), at noon rain
washes away the snow, and in the evening, as the sun goes
down and I'm standing on the bank watching a boat struggle
against the current, rain and sleet come down together . . .
And a thing occurs that doesn't go with snow and cold: I
clearly hear a peal of thunder. The coachmen cross themselves
and say it's going to be warm.

The boat is a big one. They load her first with about six
hundredweight of mail, then put in my luggage, and cover it
all with wet matting . . . The postal driver, a tall elderly man,
sits on the mail, and I sit on my trunk. At my feet a little
soldier has settled down, his face a mass of freckles. Although
his overcoat is tightly buttoned, water runs down his neck
from his cap.

"Gentlemen, cast off!"

We sail with the tide, near clumps of rose willow. The oarsmen say that only ten minutes ago two horses were drowned,
and a boy who was sitting on a cart only saved himself by
clutching at a branch of willow.

"Row, lads, row! Talk later!" says the helmsman. "Put your
backs into it!"

Along the river, as if before a storm, blow gusts of wind . . .
A bare willow leans rustling over the water and the river
suddenly darkens, and rough waves rise and fall . . .

"Swing into the bushes, lads," says the helmsman quietly.
"We'll have to wait."

We have already turned into a clump of willow, and someone remarks that, if the weather stays bad, we'll be stuck here
all night, and drown anyway in the end, so why not press on?
By a majority of voices we decide to press on . . .

The river darkens, strong wind and rain batter us from the
side, the other shore is still far off and the willows in which
we could have sheltered are some way behind us . . . The postal
driver seems to be dreaming, his eyes closed. He does not stir,

as if frozen. The oarsmen also are silent. I see that the little soldier's neck is turning crimson. My heart is full of foreboding, and I think only of this: that, if the boat capsizes, I'll fling off first my sheepskin coat, then my jacket, then . . .

But the shore comes nearer and nearer, the oarsmen pull with stronger will; little by little my foreboding falls away, and when we're no more than five yards from the shore, I suddenly become light-hearted and cheerful and I think:

"It's not too bad being a coward. You only need to wait a little and suddenly all is splendid!"

15th May

7

I do not like it when an educated man in exile stands at a window and stares silently at the roof of the house next door. What are his thoughts then? I do not like it when he chats with me about trivialities and looks into my face with an expression which says: "You will go home, but I will not." For then I feel terribly sorry for him.

The statement, often heard, that the death penalty is the exception, is not quite accurate; the other punitive measures which replaced the death penalty exercise a similar effect— for really a life sentence is an eternity—and their purpose, like that of the death penalty, is the removal of a criminal from human society *for ever*; so that a man who has committed a crime is as dead to the district where he was born and grew up, as he was when the death penalty was the rule. In our Russian legislation, in contrast to humane ones, the heaviest criminal sentences are almost always for life. Hard prison labour is invariably part of a deportation sentence. Exile is terrible because it is life-long. A man condemned to be a convict, if society will not accept him in its ranks, has to be sent to Siberia for probably the rest of his days. That the new measures do not send a criminal to eternal rest in a tomb would satisfy my opposition to the death penalty, but life imprisonment—the knowledge that all hope is gone, that as a citizen you are dead and nothing you can do will change it—this situation makes me believe that the death penalty has not been abolished but has only been modified into a less disgusting form. Europe has known the death penalty too long to reject it without long and exhausting delays.

I am deeply convinced that, in fifty to one hundred years' time, they will look back on life sentences with the bewilderment and incomprehension with which we now regard slitting of noses and cutting off a finger of the left hand. And I am also deeply convinced that, in so far as we are unable, however sincerely, to recognize the outlandishness and barbarity of things like the life sentence, we will never be able to alleviate misfortune. At the present time we have neither the knowledge nor experience nor even the courage to change the life sentence into something more rational and just; for all attempts to do so are hesitant and one-sided and can only lead to serious mistakes and excesses—such is the lot of all endeavours not based on knowledge and experience. It is strange and sad, but we have no right to decide a question so important to Russia—shall it be prison or exile?—for we are completely unaware what prison or exile really mean. Look at our literature on the subject: how paltry it is! Two or three articles, two or three names, and nothing else. As if in Russia we didn't have prisons or exile or penal servitude. For twenty, or thirty years intellectuals have been repeating the phrase that all criminals are products of society, yet how indifferent they are to those products! The cause of this indifference to those who are imprisoned or tortured in exile, incomprehensible in a Christian country and in Christian literature, is the extreme ignorance of the Russian judge. He knows so little, can no more free himself from the prejudices of his profession, than the petty clerks he mocks. He takes examinations at university to know how to sit in judgement on a man and sentence him; he joins the judiciary and receives a salary, and then he gives judgement, but where the criminal goes after trial, what prison and Siberia means, he does not know. It does not interest him or come within his competence: all that is left to the red-nosed prison guards!

According to the common people here—clerks, coachmen, waggoners—with whom I've spoken, the middle class exiles—all these ex-officers, civil servants, notaries, accountants, specimens of golden youth, sent here for forgery, embezzlement, swindling and so on—live reserved and modest lives. The exceptions are those citizens with a particularly stubborn temperament; whatever their age or circumstances they always remain themselves; but they do not stay in one place, for in Siberia they live so much like nomads and gypsies that they almost elude observation. Apart from these people, you occasionally meet middle class exiles who are deeply corrupted and immoral, scoundrels, in fact: but it is plain what they are, everyone knows and points them out. The great majority, I repeat, live modestly.

When exiles arrive in Siberia, they are bewildered and stunned: cowed, as if they have been beaten. Most of them are poor, weak and badly educated. Their only accomplishment is that they can write, which is often of little use to them. Some begin selling, one after the other, their Dutch-linen shirts, their bed-sheets, their headscarves; and two or three years later they die in terrible penury. (As Kusoblev died not long ago in Tomsk, who played a prominent part in the development of the Taganrog Customs House: his funeral was paid for by a fine and generous man who was also an exile.) Others gradually manage to get some work and find their feet; they become traders, advocates, local journalists, clerks and so on. Their earnings rarely exceed thirty to thirty-five roubles a month.

Their lives are boring. Siberian landscape, compared with Russian, seems to them monotonous, barren and insipid; frost sets in by Ascension Day and by Whitsun the damp snow is falling. Flats in the towns are foul, the streets filthy, and prices are high in the shops, nothing is fresh, and much that a European is accustomed to cannot be found for love nor money. The native middle class, whether they use their brains or not, drink vodka from morning till night, drink disgustingly, crudely and stupidly, with no restraint but without getting drunk; after the first couple of sentences one of them invariably asks: "Won't you drink vodka with us?" And out of boredom an exile drinks with him, at first with a frown, then he becomes used to it and in the end, of course, is a drunkard. In drunkenness it is not the exiles who corrupt the natives, the natives corrupt the exiles. A woman here is as boring as the landscape; she is colourless and cold, does not know how to dress, and neither sings nor laughs; she isn't pretty and, as one old fellow put it to me, is "rigid to the touch." When, as time passes, there are native novelists and poets in Siberia, woman will not be the heroine of their novels and poems; she will neither inspire them nor excite them to high endeavour, neither redeem them, nor go with them to the ends of the earth. If you discount the awful taverns, the family bath-houses and the brothels, open or furtive, to which a Siberian man is so addicted, there are no entertainments in the towns. On long autumn and winter evenings the exile sits at home or goes to an old local man and drinks with him. They drink two bottles of vodka together and half a dozen beers, and then comes the usual question: "Let's go *there*, shall we?" To a brothel. Misery upon misery! What food for the soul is here? An exile will read some worthless book like Ribeau's *The Pains of Freedom*, or on the first sunny day will put on light trousers—but that's all. Ribeau is boring, and why read about "the pains of freedom," if you have no freedom. It's cold when first you wear light trousers, but at least it makes a change.

18th May

8

The Siberian Highway is the longest and, it seems, the ugliest highway in the world. From Tyumen to Tomsk, thanks not to those who manage it but to natural conditions, it is still tolerable. The region is a flat plain without forests; rain fell this morning but now by evening it is dry; and if until the end of May the highway is covered with hills of ice, left by melting snow, you can make your way over open country by round-about tracks. Beyond Tomsk the taiga and hills begin; the earth does not dry quickly here, it's useless to seek roundabout tracks, you just have to keep to the highway. That it is why it is only after Tomsk that travellers start to grumble and write diligently in the complaint books. Those who look after the highway read through these complaints then write on each of them: "No action taken." Why bother to write? In China they would use a rubber stamp.

Two lieutenants and an army doctor travel with me from Tomsk to Irkutsk. One lieutenant is in the infantry and wears a shaggy hat, the other is a surveyor with braid on his shoulders. At each staging post, dirty, wet and sleepy, wearied by the slow pace and continual shaking, we fall into sofas and grumble: "What a lousy, horrible road!" But the station clerks and the managers tell us:

"This is nothing. Wait till you get to Kosulkoe!"

They frighten us with Kosulkoe at every staging post after Tomsk. The clerks smile mysteriously and travellers on the way back say with malice: "I went through it, thank God, now it's your turn!" And they so alarm the imagination that Kosulkoe begins to shape itself in dreams as a bird with long claws and green eyes.

They call Kosulkoe the distance of some fifteen miles between Chernorechenskoe staging post and that at Kosulkoe itself (which lies between Achinsk and Krasnoyarsk). At two or three staging posts before the terrible place, the forebodings begin. You meet a traveller who says he toppled over four times there, another who says that his axle broke, and a third who stays sullenly silent, and, when you ask him if the road's all right, replies: "Oh yes, it's all right, the devil take it!" They look at me with pity as if at a dead man, because I have my own carriage.

"It'll break down, you know, and tip you in the mud," they tell me with a sigh. "You ought to travel in a postal carriage!"

The nearer to Kosulkoe, the more terrible the forebodings. Not far from Chernorechenskoe staging post, in the evening, the carriage of my fellow-travellers suddenly topples over and the lieutenants and the doctor and their trunks and parcels, swords and a violin-case tumble into the mud. That night it's my turn. Just as we reach the staging post, my coachman announces that the "cooking piece" has given way. (This is an iron bolt connecting the front of the carriage to the axle-tree: when it gives way, the carriage bellies down on the ground.) At the staging post the repairs begin. Five coachmen, smelling stiflingly of garlic and onion, pull my carriage on its side and start to knock out the broken bolt with a hammer. They tell me that some sort of nut has cracked, a coupling has fallen, and three screws have come off; but I don't understand and don't want to . . . It's dark and cold and I'm sleepy and very bored . . .

In a room at the staging post a little lamp burns dimly. There are smells of kerosene, garlic and onion. The lieutenant in the Astrakhan hat lies sleeping on a sofa; on another a bearded man is lazily pulling on his boots: he's just received an order to go and repair a telegraph pole, but he'd much prefer to sleep. The lieutenant with braid on his shoulders and the doctor sit at a table, lay their heavy heads on their hands and doze. I hear the snores of the sleeping lieutenant and the hammering outside.

What a lot of talk there is at the staging posts! And all the talk the length of the highway comes in the end to a single theme: they criticize the local management and curse the highway itself. The telegraph service bears the brunt because it is supposed to be in charge but, in fact, does very little. To an exhausted traveller with more than 700 miles before him on the way to Irkutsk, this talk is just horrifying. He hears how a member of the Geographical Society, travelling with his wife, broke down twice and had to spend a night in the forest; how a lady had her head cracked open by the jolting; how an exciseman was stuck 16 hours in the mud and gave peasants 25 roubles to pull him out and drag him to the staging post; how not a single carriage comes through unscathed—it all echoes in the mind like the cries of an evil bird.

To judge by the talk, the postal service is the greatest sufferer. Find a good man to observe the postal traffic from Perm as far as Irkutsk and record his impressions, and you will have a story to bring tears to the eyes. To start with, those leather packages and parcels, fruitlessly destined to bring to Siberia religion, enlightenment, trade, order and money, they all have to wait a full twenty-four hours for no good reason, because the laggard steamers never reach the train on time. From Tyumen to Tomsk, in the spring until June, they have to fight with monstrous river floods and quagmires of mud; I recall that at one staging post I had to wait about a whole day and night because of floods, and the postal service waited with me. Across rivers and flooded fields heavy postal baggage goes on little boats, which only avoid capsizing, it seems, because Siberian postal carriers pray so fervently in the name of their mothers. Between Tomsk and Irkutsk the postal wagons are stuck in the mud for some ten to twenty hours at places like Kosulkoe and Chernorechenskoe, which are countless. On the 27th May at a posting stage they told me that, not long before, a bridge collapsed under a postal wagon and the horses and driver nearly drowned. That is only one of the typical misfortunes to which the postal service has long been accustomed. While I was travelling to Irkutsk over a period of six days, the post from Moscow did not overtake me; that means it was more than a week late, and all that week encountered typical misfortunes.

The Siberian postal workers are martyrs. They carry a heavy cross: heroes whom a stubborn father has no wish to recognize. They labour hard, they struggle against nature as no one else does, at times suffering unbearably, yet they are dismissed, demoted or punished much more often than they are rewarded. Do you know the wages they get, and have you ever in your life seen a postal worker wearing a medal? It may well be they are much more valuable than those who write: "No action taken"; but look at them, how downtrodden and timid they seem in your presence! . . .

But now at last they tell me my carriage is ready. I can go ahead.

"Up you get!" The doctor wakes the sleeping lieutenant. "The sooner we're through this cursed Kosulkoe, the better!"

"Gentlemen, the devil is not as black as he's painted," the bearded man consoles us. "Kosulkoe is really no worse than the other posting stages. And if you're afraid, well, you can walk the sixteen miles . . ."

"Oh yes, if you don't get stuck in the mud!" adds a clerk.

Dawn glimmers in the sky. It is cold . . . The coachmen have not even left the courtyard but they're saying: "Not this road, oh, God forbid!" We go first through a village . . . Our wheels sink in liquid mud, or bump over hummocks or into pot-holes; the logged tracks and pontoon bridges are sinking into the liquid mud, and beams are sticking out like ribs, so that a traveller's blood runs cold and axles break . . .

But we get through the village and are in the dreaded Ko-sulkoe. The road is certainly awful but I don't find it worse, for example, than the one near Marinsk or at Chernorechenskoe itself. Imagine for yourself a broad swathe through a landscape along which runs an embankment about ten yards wide—that's the highway. If you look at the embankment from the side, you see a huge ridge rise from the earth. On both sides of it are ditches. Along the ridge run ruts about three feet deep, but a mass of others cut across, so that the ridge looks like a chain of mountains with Caucasian peaks among them. The summits have already dried out and knock against the wheels but water slops about in the valleys. Only an adept juggler of a coachman can drive his carriage along this embankment and keep it upright. Usually the carriage tilts at such an unusual angle that you shout: "Coachman, we're turning over." Some-times the right wheels sink in a deep rut, while the left wheels are on a summit; or two wheels are stuck in mud, a third is on a summit, and a fourth hangs in the air . . . A carriage may take thousands of positions, and you clutch your head, then your side, bite your tongue and swing about in all directions, while your trunks and boxes bang against each other and against you. And you look at the coachman: how does that acrobat manage to stay on his box?

If someone watched as we go by, he would say we are crazy people, not travellers. We want to keep away from the ridge of the embankment and move to the side, trying to find an easier way ahead, but we come upon ruts, hummocks and potholes. We struggle on a little, then the coachman halts; he ponders for a minute, then, grunting helplessly, and with the expression of one about to play a dirty trick, drives straight towards a ditch. There is tremendous noise: the front wheels crack, the back wheels crack—and we are over the ditch. Then we go up the embankment, with more cracking and crashing. Sweat drips from the horses, harness tears, shaft traces ravel out and fray. "Mother of God!" shouts the coachman, whipping them with all his strength. "Come on, lads, devil take you!" They drag their burden about ten paces, then stop; and no amount of whipping and cursing can make them go further. There is nothing for it but to come down and make for the ditch again, seek an easier way again, ponder once more, then go back up the ridge—and so on and on, endlessly.

It is hard to keep going, very hard, but it becomes harder still when you realise that this ugly rippling strip of land, this black mess is almost the only artery that links Europe and Siberia! And along this artery to Siberia, they say, flows civilization. Oh yes, they say that; they say a great deal; but if the coachmen and the postal drivers should overhear them, and the carriers, soaked to the skin and up to their knees in mud beside their line of carts that bring tea to Europe, what opinion would they have of Europe and European integrity?

Look at the line of carts, then. Some forty of them, with chests of tea, a line that stretches along the embankment . . . The wheels are half-hidden in deep ruts, the emaciated little

horses strain their necks . . . Beside the carts the carters trudge
along, dragging heavy feet through the mud and helping on
the horses. They have long been at the point of collapse. See,
a part of the line has halted. What's wrong? A wheel of one of
the carts has broken . . . No, better not look too closely.

As if in mockery of these coachmen, postal drivers, carriers
and horses, someone has had piles of brick rubbish and stones
set up at the sides of the highway. To remind them every
minute that soon the road will get even worse. They say that
in towns and villages along the Siberian Highway live people
who receive salaries for keeping it in repair. If that is true,
they should have a rise in pay, lest, God help us, they work
too hard, for repair work only makes things worse and worse.
Peasants say that, when the highway is repaired in a place like
Kosulkoe, this is what happens. At the end of June or the
beginning of July, in the high season of clouds of mosquitoes—
a time of Oriental torture—they drive people from their villages and set them to fill dried-up ruts and pot-holes with
brushwood and rubbishy brick and stone which crumbles into
dust between the fingers; this repair work goes on until the
end of summer. Then the snow comes and covers the highway
with bumps and hollows unique in the world, which make
you seasick as you go along—then spring again and mud, the
repair work again—and so on and on from year to year.

On the way to Tomsk I became acquainted with an inspector of highways and travelled with him over two or three
staging posts. I recall that we were sitting in a log cabin belong-
ing to a Jew and eating perch, when someone came and reported that a part of the highway was in a state of ruin and
that the contractor didn't want to do anything about it . . .

"Send him to me!" ordered the inspector.

After a time a little man came in, dishevelled, with a twisted
face. The inspector leapt from his chair and went for him.

"How dare you refuse to repair the highway, you scoundrel?" he shouted in a whining voice. "It's impossible to travel
on it, people break their necks, the governor writes about it,
so does the district police officer, I take the blame, whereas

you, you blackguard, devil take your hide . . . what are you looking at? Oh, you reptile! Have the highway repaired by tomorrow! I'll come back then and if I find the highway still unrepaired, I'll cripple you, you criminal! Get to work!"

The little man blinked his eyes, broke out in a sweat, twisted his already twisted face and rushed out. The inspector returned to his table, sat down and said with a smile:

"Of course, compared with those from Petersburg and Moscow, our local ladies may not please you, but look carefully and you can find a nice girl here . . ."

It would be interesting to know what the little man managed to do by the following day. What could he achieve in that short time? I do not know whether it is good or bad for the highway that inspectors do not stay long in one place, they are always moving them about. They say that one recently appointed inspector, arriving in his district, ordered out the peasants to dig ditches at the side of the highway; his successor, eager not to yield to him in originality, made the peasants fill the ditches in. A third ordered them to cover the highway with clay to a depth of twelve inches. A fourth, fifth, sixth and seventh—they all tried to bring into the hive their little dollop of honey . . .

Throughout the year the highway remains in a terrible state; mud in spring; in summer dried-up ruts and pot-holes and repair work; in winter bumps and hollows. Those swift Siberian sleigh-rides which enthralled the imaginations of F. F. Vigel and later of I. A. Goncharov are really only possible in the first snows of winter. It is true that contemporary writers are full of enthusiasm for swift Siberian sleigh-rides, but that is because, once in Siberia, it would be awkward for them not to experience such rides, if only in imagination.

I find it difficult to hope that sometime Kosulkoe will stop breaking axles and wheels. The Siberian officials have seen no better roads this century; they like that state of affairs, and the complaint books and the critical letters from travellers do no more good than the money set aside for road repair . . .

We reach the Kosulkoe staging post when the sun is already

high. My fellow travellers continue their journey, but I stay
behind for my carriage to be repaired.

9

If the landscape from Russia into Siberia has not appealed to
you, you will have a further boring time from the Urals as far
as the Yenisey. A cold plain, twisted birch trees, pools and
puddles, scattered lakes, snow in May and a wilderness still,
the sullen banks of tributaries of the Ob—that is all the memory retains of the first 1500 miles. The landscape which non-
natives idealize and Russians who pass through esteem, and
which in time will be an inexhaustible gold mine for Siberian
poets, a landscape unique, majestic and beautiful—that only
begins with the Yenisey.

I have to say, with no malice to jealous admirers of the
Volga, that never in my life have I seen a more splendid river
than the Yenisey. The Volga, I concede, is an elegant, modest
and melancholy beauty, but the Yenisey is a fierce and mighty
warrior who knows not what to do with his power and his
youth. Man set out boldly along the Volga but ended with a
moan that is called song, his bright golden hopes turned to a
sickness we are pleased to call "Russian pessimism"; life began with a moan along the Yenisey but will end with an
audacity we have only seen in dreams. At least it seemed so
to me as I stood on the shore of the immense Yenisey and
looked eagerly at the waters which rushed along with terrible
speed and power towards the stern Arctic Ocean. There is a
tension on the shores of the Yenisey. Low waves pursue each
other, crowd together and make spiralling whirlpools, and it
seems strange that this Hercules does not wash away the
banks and undermine them. Krasnoyarsk is on one shore, the
finest and most beautiful of all Siberian cities, and there are
hills over there that remind me of the Caucasus, they are so
smoky and dream-like. I stood and reflected: how rich and
wise and daring will be the life that one day these shores will
see. I envied the Siberian, who, as I read, is sailing by steamship

from Petersburg to the Arctic Ocean, and then will make his way to the estuary of the Yenisey; I regret that a university has opened at Tomsk and not there at Krasnoyarsk. Many and various were my thoughts, which merged and clustered like the waters of the Yenisey, and I felt good . . .

Soon after the Yenisey the famous taiga begins. So much has been written and spoken about it that you expect more than it can give; and at first you are somewhat disappointed. Along both sides of the highway there stretch without a break some commonplace forests of pine, larch, fir and birch. There are no trees that are five times thicker than you can grasp, no tree-tops to make your head swim at the sight; the trees, in fact, are no bigger than those which grow in the Sokolnik region of Moscow province. They told me the taiga was silent and its vegetation had no smell. I expected to find it so, but, all the time I travelled through the taiga, birds poured out their song, insects droned, branches of conifers, warmed by the sun, drenched the air with a dense smell of resin, and glades and borders of the highway were covered with soft-blue, pink and yellow flowers, which pleased more than the eye. Clearly, those who wrote about the taiga did not observe it in spring but in summer, when, in Russia too, the forests are silent and have no smell.

The power and fascination of the taiga are not in giant trees and deep silence but in the fact that only birds of passage know where it ends. In the first day you pay no attention to this; in the second and third you are surprised, but in the fourth and fifth your spirits sink to such a point that you feel you will never escape the clutches of this monster of the earth. You scramble up a high hill, surrounded by forest, you stare ahead to the east along the route of the highway, and see forest below you, a hill further off, trees clustering to the top, then another wooded hill, then a third, and so endlessly on. Next day you stare ahead from another hill—and the picture is the same . . . You know, of course, that Angara and Irkutsk are in that direction, but what are beyond the hills that stretch north and south of the highway, and how many hundreds of miles they stretch, not even the coachmen and the local peasants know. Their imaginations are bolder than ours, but they have decided to set no random limit to the taiga, and, when you ask, they say: "There's no end to it!" They only know that in winter people from the far north cross the taiga with reindeer and buy bread, but what kind of people they are, and where they come from, even old-timers do not know.

Over there near some pine trees a fugitive drags himself along, a knapsack and a kettle at his back. How petty in this enormous taiga seem his furtiveness, his sufferings and himself! He will perish and it will seem no more strange and terrible than the death of a midge. With such a sparse population the taiga is strong and unconquerable, and the phrase: "Man is the lord of nature"—sounds nowhere so shallow and false as here. If, let's imagine, all the people along the Siberian Highway decided to subdue the taiga and set to work with axes and fire, they would repeat the legend of the bluebird that tried to set fire to the sea. It happens that fire burns down the forest over a distance of three miles, but the scorched earth is scarcely noticed in the vast mass, and a young forest grows there, thicker and darker than the old. A scientist who worked at the eastern edge of the taiga started a forest fire by accident: in a moment all the visible green mass was engulfed in flames. Horrified by what he saw, the scientist proclaimed that he was "the cause of a terrible calamity." But what in the enormous-spreading taiga are some ten miles of fire? In fact, in the place of that fire an impenetrable forest is now growing, bears wander tranquilly, hazel grouse fly, and the scientist's work has had greater effect on nature than the terrible calamity he feared. The usual measures that men take have unexpected results in the taiga.

How many secrets the taiga hides! There, among the trees, a winding track disappears in forest twilight. Where does it go? To a secret distillery, or a village unknown to the police or the inspector of highways, or perhaps a gold mine discovered by an association of tramps? What a seductive air of freedom these mysterious paths have!

According to the coachmen, there are bears, wolves, stags, sable foxes and wild goats in the taiga. Men who live along the highway, when there's no work to do at home, go off for weeks on end to shoot wild animals. The art of hunting is very simple here: if the rifle doesn't go off or misfires, you have to plead for mercy from a bear. One hunter complained to me that his rifle misfired five times in succession; to go hunting with a man like that, unless you have a knife or pike, is a terrible risk. Imported rifles are poor and also dear, so that along the highway you often find blacksmiths who know how to make rifles. For the most part they are talented people, these blacksmiths, and this is appreciated here because their particular talents are not lost among a mass of others. Once I made the brief acquaintance of a blacksmith whom my coachman recommended with these words. "Oh, he's a master of his craft! He can even make rifles!" And his tone and the expression on his face made me vividly remember people talking about great artists. My carriage had broken down, it had to be repaired, and, recommended by my coachman, there came from the staging post a pale, lean man with nervous movements, to all appearances a great and gifted drinker. Like a good practising doctor, who is bored to treat an uninteresting disease, he gave my carriage a cursory and reluctant glance, made a brief and sharp diagnosis, and, without a word to me, sauntered along the road, then looked back and told my coachman:

"All right, then! Bring the carriage to the smithy!"

Four joiners helped him to repair the carriage. He worked carelessly, reluctantly, and it seemed the iron took diverse forms against his will; he smoked a lot, burrowed for no good reason into a pile of iron debris, and, when I tried to hurry him, looked up into the sky—thus do artists behave when called upon to sing or read a work. From time to time, in affectation, or to impress me and the joiners, he lifted his hammer high, sent sparks flying in all directions and with a single blow resolved some deep and complicated question. By this rough and heavy blow, from which, it seemed the anvil would break and the earth shake, the iron took a required shape, so that not even a flea could raise objections. He received from me five and a half roubles for the work; he kept the five and gave the half to the joiners. These men said thank you, and dragged the carriage to the staging post, clearly envious of a talent that knows its worth, and is as despotic in the taiga as in any of our big cities.

20th June

1890

CHEKHOV'S LIFE, WORK
AND CONTEMPORARY EVENTS

❖ ❖ ❖

Date	Life	Events	Work
1860	Anton born in Taganrog, 17th January.		
1862		Turgenev's *Fathers and Sons* is published.	
1863		The abolition of serfdom. Anton's grandfather had been a serf.	
1866		Dostoevsky's *Crime and Punishment* is published.	
1867	Anton attends a school at the Church of St. Constantine.		
1869	Anton enters Taganrog Grammar School.	Tolstoy's *War and Peace* is published.	

Date	Life	Events	Work
1876	Anton's father's business collapses and the family moves to Moscow. Anton has to support himself in Taganrog for the next three years.		
1877		Tolstoy's *Anna Karenina* is published.	
1879	Anton passes his matriculation examination on July 15th. In August Anton joins his family in Moscow and becomes a medical student at Moscow University.		
1880	To pay for his studies and to support his family Anton Chekhov writes for humorous journals.	Dostoevsky's *The Brothers Karamazov* is published.	Anton Chekhov's first story is published.
1881		Death of Dostoevsky.	
1882		The Czar Alexander the Second is assassinated. Alexander the Third repudiates his father's reforms.	"Two Scandals" "He and She"
1883		Death of Turgenev.	"The Crooked Mirror" "A Woman Without Prejudices" "He Understood"

Date	Life	Events	Work
1884	Chekhov obtains his degree of Doctor of Medicine. He works as a doctor.		"75,000" "Tears the World Does Not See" "The Mask" "A Terrible Night"
1885			"The Crow" "The Boots" "The Father of a Family" "The Exclamation Mark" "The Dream" "The Mirror"
1886			"Misery" "A Night in the Graveyard" "The Wolf" "The Trick" "Agafya" "A Gentleman Friend" "Love Affair with a Double-Bass" Ivanov (play)
1887	Chekhov is awarded the Pushkin Prize by the Russian Academy of Sciences.		"Sleepy" "Steppe" "The Beauties" "Lights" The Bear (one-act play)
1889	Chekhov is elected a member of the Society of Lovers of Russian Literature.		"A Boring Story" The Wood Demon (play) The Proposal (one-act play)

Date	Life	Events	Work
1890	In April, May and June Chekhov crosses Siberia. In July he arrives at Sakhalin Island. He makes a survey of convict settlements. He returns home by way of Hong Kong, Singapore and Ceylon.		*From Siberia*
			"Gusev"
1891	He makes a journey to Western Europe, visits Vienna, Venice, Florence, Rome, Nice, Paris.		"The Duel" "The Women"
1892	Chekhov works on famine relief in Novgorod province. He buys a farm at Melikhovo south of Moscow and moves there with all his family. He fights a cholera epidemic there.		"The Grasshopper" "Ward No. 6" "In Exile" "Neighbours"
1893			*Sakhalin Island* "The Chorus Girl"
1894	Chekhov goes on holiday to Italy.	Alexander the Third dies. He is succeeded by Nicholas the Second.	"The Black Monk" "Women's Kingdom" "The Student"
1895			"The House with the Mezzanine" "Three Years" "Murder" *The Seagull* (play)

Date	Life	Events	Work
1896	Chekhov visits the Caucasus and the Crimea.		*My Life*
1897	Chekhov falls seriously ill. Consumption is diagnosed. He goes to the south of France for the winter.		"Peasants" "In the Cart"
1898	Chekhov's father dies. He buys land and builds a house at Yalta.		"The Man in a Case" "The Darling" *Uncle Vanya* (play)
1899	Chekhov sells his farm and moves with his family to Yalta.		"The Lady with the Little Dog" "In the Ravine"
1900	Chekhov is elected a member of the Russian Academy of Sciences.		*The Three Sisters* (play)
1901	On May 25th Anton Chekhov marries Olga Knipper, an actress of the Moscow Art Theatre.		
1902	Chekhov resigns from the Academy of Sciences as a protest against the rejection of Maxim Gorki. Olga has a miscarriage.		"The Bishop"
1903	Chekhov's health deteriorates.		"The Bride" *The Cherry Orchard* (play)

Date	Life	Events	Work
1904	Chekhov and his wife go to Badenweiler, a German health resort. It is the beginning of June. On July 2nd Chekhov dies at Badenweiler.